Did You
Ever Have
a Family

Center Point
Large Print

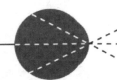

**This Large Print Book carries the
Seal of Approval of N.A.V.H.**

Did You Ever Have a Family

BILL CLEGG

CENTER POINT LARGE PRINT
THORNDIKE, MAINE

This Center Point Large Print edition
is published in the year 2015 by arrangement with
Scout Press, a division of Simon & Schuster, Inc.

The text of this Large Print edition is unabridged.
In other aspects, this book may vary
from the original edition.
Printed in the United States of America
on permanent paper.
Set in 16-point Times New Roman type.

ISBN: 978-1-62899-751-4

Library of Congress Cataloging-in-Publication Data

Clegg, Bill.
  Did you ever have a family / Bill Clegg. — Center Point Large Print
edition.
    pages cm
  ISBN 978-1-62899-751-4 (library binding : alk. paper)
  I. Title.
  PS3603.L455447D53 2015b
  813´.6—dc23
                                                    2015027922

For Van, and for our families

You should have
    heard him,
        his voice was
unforgettable, irresistible, his voice
was an imaginary garden woven through
    with fragrance.

Did you ever have a family?
        Their eyes are closed.
That's how I know
    we're there
        inside it,
it's made of sound and steam
that weaves between dark
dining room, bright kitchen.
We're there because I'm hungry,
and we'll all be eating soon
        together, and the hunger's sweet

—Alan Shapiro,
"Song and Dance"

Silas

He wakes to the sound of sirens. Many, loud, and very near. Then horns: short, angry grunts like the buzzers signaling time-out in the basketball games he watches but does not play in at school. His cell phone says 6:11 a.m., but the house downstairs is awake and loud and from the particular pitch of his mother's rough morning voice, scratching above his father's and sisters', he knows something is wrong.

Before he kicks off the covers, Silas grabs his yellow knapsack from under the bed. He pulls out the small, red bong his friend Ethan gave him last month for his fifteenth birthday along with a bag of pot he smoked in less than a week, mostly on the job yanking weeds from flower beds and patios for rich New Yorkers. He selects a green bud from the small, gray Tupperware container where he keeps his stash, carefully pinches it in half, and presses the larger piece into the metal bowl. He grabs the half-filled water bottle sitting on his nightstand and pours a few inches into the bong before lighting. As he inhales, he notices the smoke curl toward his mouth, thicken in the red tube, and turn, slowly, like a sheet twisting underwater. Once the bud has mostly turned to ash, he pulls the stem from the bong and releases the smoke to his lungs. The water gurgles at the bong's base, and he is careful to inhale gently to minimize the noise. He opens the window, snaps off the screen, and leans out, exhaling in one full, sloppy breath.

He watches the smoke float before him, catch the wind, vanish. He feels the cool air against his face and neck and waits for the pot to work its magic. The sky is pink and pale blue, and he traces a long trail of plane exhaust above him until it disappears over the roofline of the garage. The streaks are fluffy and loose, and so he thinks the plane must have flown over hours ago, before daybreak. To where? he wonders, the drug beginning to lozenge his thoughts.

Below him, four beefy crows land gracelessly on the lawn. He watches them hop and step and tuck their wings into their chest-thick bodies. They are the size of house cats, he thinks as he follows their quick, mechanical movements. After a while and for no apparent reason, they stop and stand perfectly still. He cannot see their eyes, but he senses they are staring up at him. He stares back. They cock their heads from side to side as if making sense of what they see. Wind ruffs their feathers from behind, and after a few hops they take flight. Airborne, they appear even larger, and for the first time he considers whether they might be hawks, or vultures. Then, as if unmuted, birds of all kinds squawk and screech and chirp from every direction. Startled, Silas knocks the back of his head against the top of the window. He rubs the spot and leans farther out. Another siren, different from the others—higher pitched, more upset—screams from far off. He tries to locate the crows that have disappeared into the complicated morning sky. What he finds instead are familiar shapes in the streaks and billows: a mountainous pair of swelling breasts, cat-eyed sunglasses, a fiery bird with vast wings. Then he sees what looks like nothing but what it is: smoke, pitch-black and thick, rising behind the roofline. At first he thinks his house is on fire, but when he leans out and looks back, he can see that the smoke is coming from beyond the trees on the other side of the property. Then he smells it—the oily stench of a fire burning more than just wood. He can taste it, too, and as he inhales, it mingles with the pot smoke still on his tongue and in his throat. The birds get louder. Squawking, yelling what sound like words. *Go! You! Go!* he thinks he hears, but knows it's impossible. He blinks his eyes open and shut, attempts to process each thing: the smoke, the smell, the birds, the sirens, the magnificent sky. Is he dreaming? Is this a nightmare? Is it the pot? He got it from Tess at the farm stand up the road, and her stuff is usually mellow, not like the trippy buds he and his friends drive an hour and a half south to score in Yonkers. He wishes he were having a nightmare or hallucinating, but he knows he's awake and what he sees is real.

At the tree line on the other side of the house, smoke pumps into the sky like pollution from a cartoon smokestack. It puffs and thins, puffs and thins. Then a terrible cloud, larger than the rest, swells from the same unseen source. It is dense, coal black, and faintly silver at the edges. As it rises, it expands into a greenish gray and then dissolves into a long, crooked wisp that points across the sky like the worst finger.

Silas backs away from the window. Still wearing the shorts and T-shirt from the night before, he slips on his old, gray-and-white New Balance running shoes, the ones he wears when he works his landscaping jobs or stacks firewood with his father. He looks in the mirror above his dresser and sees that his eyes are pinkish, bulging slightly, and his pupils are dilated. His unwashed-for-days, dark blond hair is jagged and oily, flat to his head in some places, standing on end in others. He rubs a stick of deodorant on his armpits and puts on his black, corduroy, Mohawk Mountain ski cap. He swigs the remaining water from the bottle by the bed and shoves a few sticks of Big Red gum in his mouth. He grabs the yellow knapsack and packs up his bong, his lighter, and the small Tupperware container. He rubs his eyes with both fists, breathes in deeply, exhales, and steps toward his bedroom door.

His thumb and forefinger graze the knob, and he remembers the night before, where he was and what happened. He steps back, traces his last movements before falling asleep, runs through it all once and then again to make sure it is not a dream he is remembering. He considers and then dismisses the possibility of taking another bong hit before leaving his room. He stands still, speaks to himself in a whisper. *I'm okay. Everything's okay. Nothing's happened.*

Downstairs, his mother's iPhone rings innocently, like an old-fashioned phone. She answers on the third ring and the house falls silent. The only sounds now are the tireless sirens, the grunting horns, and the distant hum of helicopter blades beating the air. From the kitchen, his father shouts his name. Silas steps away from the door.

June

She will go. Tuck into her Subaru wagon and roll down these twisting, potholed country roads until she finds a highway, points west and away. She will keep going for as long and as far as possible without a passport, since the one she had no longer exists. Her driver's license, along with everything else that had been in the house, is also gone, but she figures she won't need it unless she is pulled over for speeding. She had not planned on leaving this particular morning, but after she wakes and showers and slowly puts on the jeans and blue-and-white-striped, boat-neck, cotton jersey she has been wearing for weeks, she knows it's time.

She washes and dries the chipped coffee mug, ceramic bowl, and old silver spoon she's been using since she came to this borrowed house; feels the weight of each object as she places it carefully back in the cupboard or drawer. There is nothing to pack, nothing to organize or prepare. All she has with her is the clothing on her body and the linen jacket she wore eighteen nights ago when she rushed from the house. As she slowly pushes her arms through the worn sleeves, she tries to remember why she'd put it on in the first place. Had it been cold in the kitchen? Had she pulled it from the overwhelmed coatrack by the porch door before chasing into the field, careful not to wake everyone upstairs? She can't remember; and as she starts reviewing the events of that night and the morning after, examining again each step with forensic attention, she forces herself to stop.

That she has her cash card and car keys with her is luck—they had been in the jacket pockets—but she does not think of herself as lucky. No one does. Still, these stowaways from her old life allow her now to leave town, which is all she wants. It isn't restlessness, or a desire to be somewhere else, but a blunt recognition that her time in this place has expired. *Okay,* she exhales, as if ceding a long, winless argument. She looks out the kitchen window at the orange and red daylilies blooming behind this house that is not hers. She presses her hands against the rim of the sink, and in the basement the dryer she'd filled over an hour ago with wet sheets signals its duty done with one long, harsh bleat. The porcelain feels cool under her palms. The house without sound is now loud with nothing, no one. A molten ache returns, turns in her chest, scrapes slowly. Outside, the daylilies flail in the morning wind.

She has not cried. Not that day, not at the funerals, not after. She has said little, has had few words when she needs them, so she finds herself only able to nod, shake her head, and wave the concerned and curious away as she would marauding gnats. The fire chief and police officer answered questions more than asked them—the old stove, gas leaking through the night and filling, like liquid, the first floor of the house, a spark most likely from an electric switch or a lighter, though none had been found, the explosion, the instant and all-consuming fire. They did not ask her why she was the only one outside the house at five forty-five in the morning. But when the officer asked if her boyfriend, Luke, had any reason to want to harm her or her family, she stood and walked out of the church hall, where a makeshift crisis center had been created. This is the church where her daughter, Lolly, would have been married that day; across the road and a short walk from the house. Guests had shown up before one o'clock expecting a wedding and found instead a parking lot filled with police sedans, ambulances, fire trucks, and news vans. She remembers walking out of the church toward her friend Liz, who was waiting in her car. She remembers how talk stopped and people shuffled and half stepped out of her way. She heard her name called out— timidly, unsure—but she did not stop or turn around to respond. She was, she sensed sharply as she reached the far side of the parking lot, an untouchable. Not from scorn or fear, but from the obscenity of the loss. It was inconsolable, and the daunting completeness of it—everyone, gone— silenced even those most used to calamity. She could feel all eyes on her as she opened the car door to get in. She remembers seeing in her peripheral vision a woman coming toward her, holding up her hand. Seated, she could see clearly through the car window Luke's mother, Lydia—busty, bright-bloused, long brown hair piled loosely on her head. This was the second time she'd seen her that day, and as before, despite a powerful urge to go to her, there was no way she could face the woman. *Go* was all she could say to Liz, who sat in the driver's seat spellbound and mute like everyone else in the parking lot.

The police never questioned her again about what happened that night and the following morning. Friends stopped asking her the same safe questions—was she okay, did she need anything—when she didn't respond. A thin smile, a blank stare, and turning her head away discouraged even the most persistent. A morning news anchor was especially pushy. *People want to know how you're surviving,* this woman, who had been on television since the seventies but had not one crease or line on her face, said to her in front of the funeral home. *No one survived,* she said in response, and then, quietly, *Stop,* which the woman did. Eventually, everyone who had been in town for Lolly's wedding left, the questions ended, and she was, at the age of fifty-two and for the first time in her life, alone. Through that first week and after, she refused to wail or fall apart or in any way begin a process that would bring her closer to rejoining the new and now empty world, or, as someone urged in a well-meaning but unsigned note that accompanied one of the hundreds of funeral arrangements, to *begin again.*

She buttons her jacket and starts to close and lock the windows of the small cottage loaned to her by a painter she once represented. *For as long as you need,* Maxine said that day over Liz's cell phone, *the place is yours.* Maxine was in Minneapolis, where she'd been when everything happened. How she found out so fast and knew what was needed, June still did not know. Some people, she decided, magically surface in these horrible moments knowing exactly what to do, which spaces to fill. The cottage was on the other side of Wells, the same small town in Litchfield County, Connecticut, where her house had been, where she'd come on weekends for nineteen years and had been living full-time for the last three. Maxine's dusty, little place is far away and unfamiliar enough for these weeks to be bearable. That anything could be bearable was a shameful minute-to-minute revelation. How am I here? Why? She allows these questions, but she keeps others from herself. It is safer to ask the ones she doesn't have the answers to.

She has refused to be admitted to the town hospital or to take any of the sedatives or mood stabilizers the few people around her have urged her to let them have a doctor prescribe. There is nothing to stabilize, she thinks. Nothing to be stable for. In the cottage she has slept past noon each day and after waking moved from bed to chair to kitchen table to couch and eventually back to bed again. She has occupied space, tolerated each minute until the next one arrived, and then the next.

She switches off the kitchen light, locks the front door, and places the key under the geranium pot plopped haphazardly toward the edge of the stoop. She walks from the house to her car reluctantly, recognizing that these steps are likely the last she will take in what remains of her life here. She listens for birds and, as she does, wonders what she expects to hear. Farewells? Curses? The birds see everything, she thinks, and for now they are silent. Under the high canopy of black-locust trees that stretch between the cottage and the driveway where her car is parked, there is little sound save for the faint buzz of fading cicadas, who had weeks ago emerged from their seventeen-year slumber to mate, fill the world with their electric hum, and die. Their sudden appearance had seemed like a beautiful omen the week before Lolly's wedding when the slow early-summer news cycle seemed to talk about little else. Their last gasp now seems as fitting as their arrival was then.

June rushes the last steps and yanks the driver's-side door open before slamming it shut behind her. She fiddles with the keys, unable at first to find the right one. She eyes the four on the ring as if each has betrayed her: one for the Subaru, one for the front door of her house, one for Luke's truck, and an old one she still had from her last rental in the city. She wrestles all but the Subaru key off the ring and drops them in the cup holder next to her seat. She turns the key in the ignition, and as the machine rumbles to life beneath and around her, she recognizes again that she is awake and in the world, not stumbling through some outlandish nightmare. *This is the world,* she says to herself with grim wonder, touching the steering wheel dully with her fingers.

She backs the black Subaru out of the driveway, shifts from reverse to drive, and inches slowly along the narrow dirt road until she pulls onto Route 4. She fills the gas tank at a full-service station in Cornwall and drives until merging south onto Route 7, with its swoops and curves and steep, grassy banks. On an empty stretch of road she fishes the three keys from the cup holder, opens the passenger-seat window, and in one swift motion tosses them from the car. She closes the window, presses her foot harder on the gas pedal, and speeds past two spotted fawns, stumbling several yards from their mother. For as long as she's been driving between Connecticut and Manhattan, dozens of deer have grazed alongside this stretch of road, oblivious to the speeding cars a few feet away. How many times had one darted into traffic, she thinks, imagining all the close calls—the ones she's had and the countless others everyone who's driven this road has survived, thanking God and exhaling as they sped safely away. She thinks of the unlucky souls who didn't speed away and the staggering catastrophes these stupid and beautiful creatures must have caused. She accelerates, pushing past the speed limit . . . 52, 58, 66 . . . and as the wagon shudders, she considers how many people have actually died here, their bodies dragged from twisted metal, charred into objects no longer resembling human beings. Her palms get damp against the steering wheel, and she wipes each one on her jeans. Her light jacket feels tight and constricting, but she does not want to stop the car to take it off. She passes another grouping of deer—a doe and a young buck with their spindle-legged fawn—and as she does, she imagines the wreckage: shattered glass, smoking tires, survivors identifying bodies. Her breathing is quick and shallow and she broils inside her clothes. South of Kent village she comes upon an open stretch of road, fields of summer corn fanning out in tight rows from either side. The wagon approaches 70 and the windows rattle in their wells. She imagines, with more detail than she wishes she were capable of, a sea of yellow crime scene tape, police-car and fire-engine lights, the spark and smoke of road flares, ambulances lined up with EMTs standing by, useless.

She pictures the dazed survivors, aimlessly stumbling. She circles each one, agitating with questions. Who had been driving? Who looked away at exactly the wrong instant? Who fiddled with the radio instead of paying attention? Who leaned over to find a mint in a purse, or a lighter, and by doing so lost everyone that mattered? How many, she wonders, stepped from the wreckage without a bruise or scrape? And of these lucky and living, who had been in the middle of a quarrel just before the moment of impact? Who had been fighting with someone they loved? Going at it long enough to unleash the irretrievable words they knew to say only because they had been trusted to know what would hurt the most. Words that cut quick and deep, inflicting damage that only time could repair, but now there was none. *These people,* she mutters, somewhere between curse and consolation. She can see them crouching along the roadside, doubled over and alone.

Sweat soaks her clothes and her hands tremble on the wheel. An oncoming car flashes its head-lights, and she remembers that a speeding ticket will end her flight. She has no identification, no Social Security card or birth certificate, which would be the least she'd need to secure a new driver's license. She slows the wagon to 55 and lets a green pickup truck pass. Had the driver seen the flashing headlights? Judging by how fast he was going, she doubts he had. We never pay attention to the right things, she thinks, as she watches the truck vanish beyond the bend ahead, until it's too late.

She opens her side window and air blows through the car, chilling her damp skin and tossing the shoulder-length blond and silver hair she's worn in a short ponytail and not washed for weeks. To her right, the Housatonic River snakes closely alongside the unruly road, midday sun sparking off its lazy currents. She relaxes, less from the coolness in the air and more from its turbulence. She opens the passenger-seat window and, feeling the added chaos, opens the remaining two behind her. Wind explodes through the car. She remembers Lolly's long-ago Etch A Sketch and how upset she became once when a friend shook it and the mysterious sandy insides wiped clean whatever careful scribble she had made there. She remembers Lolly's screaming—piercing, wild, indignant—and how she refused to be consoled or touched. It would be over a year before Lolly would allow that friend back for a playdate. Even young, her daughter held grudges.

June closes her eyes and imagines the wind-blasted car as an Etch A Sketch hurtling forward, the rough air wiping her clean. She hears that particular sound of shaken sand against plastic and metal, and momentarily the trick works. Her mind empties. The imagined roadside calamities and their self-pitying culprits vanish. Even Lolly—tear-streaked and furious—disappears.

June settles deeper into her seat and slows the car just below the speed limit. She passes a farm stand, a newish CVS where a video store once stood, miles of crumbling stone walls, and a dusty white house with the same pink-painted sign in front that has been there for as long as she can remember, CRYSTALS stenciled in pale blue underneath black letters that spell ROCK SHOP. For years, these were the things she saw on this drive—each marking the distance between the two lives that had for so long passed as one. She tries again to summon the Etch A Sketch— this time to erase the memory of all the giddy Friday-afternoon flights from the city and the too-soon Sunday-evening returns with Lolly in the backseat, Adam in front, driving too fast, as always, and June pivoting between them, talking about teachers and coaches at school, which movie to see that night, what to eat. Those car rides flew by and were the least complicated part of their lives. The memory of them steals her breath, surprises her with an ache for a time she almost never remembers fondly. If it could only have been as simple as that: the three of them in a car, heading home.

The river disappears from view and she slows

the car to 20 as she approaches the half-mile stretch that everyone who travels this road regularly knows is a speed trap. She crosses from Kent into New Milford and passes the McDonald's she has long considered the unofficial border between country and suburb. In the parking lot, children climb from the open doors of a dark green van like clowns out of a circus car and stand restlessly before a row of elaborate motorcycles parked in front. A young man jogs beyond them, a sturdy chocolate Lab keeping perfect pace by his side. They cross in front of an old gas station, boarded up and empty, the pumps removed. June remembers stopping there twice, maybe three times, in the years she's been driving this road but cannot remember its going out of business. Weeds have sprung up in the cracked pavement of its parking lot, and she notices the Lab circle a scruffy bunch of dandelions and grass, on which he lifts his leg and pees. His master jogs patiently in place a few yards away.

The light ahead blinks red and she slows to a halt behind another Subaru wagon, this one dark green, newer, and filled with what appear to be teenagers. She avoids looking at them and instead focuses on the blue Connecticut license plate and the Nantucket-ferry stickers peeling on the back window. A siren signaling noon sounds from a nearby fire station. It starts low and soft, like a French horn, and builds gradually to a high, wide wail so loud and overwhelming she covers her ears with the thin linen sleeves of her coat. The light finally turns green, and as it does, she closes all the windows. The bus driver behind her taps his horn—once, politely—and she eases her foot from the brake until the car begins to roll forward.

The siren dies. The air inside the car is still again. She passes restaurants and clothing stores and supermarkets she's driven past for decades but never entered. OPEN signs hang from windows, garlands of tiny, multicolored flags snap in the wind above a Cadillac dealership. Through the rearview mirror she watches it all get smaller.

Edith

They wanted daisies in jelly jars. Local daisies in fifty or so jelly jars they'd collected after they were engaged. Seemed childish to me, especially since June Reid wasn't exactly putting her daughter's wedding together on a shoestring. But who was I to have an opinion? Putting daisies in jelly jars is hardly high-level flower arranging, more like monkey work if you want to know the truth. Still, work is work, and the flower business around here is thin, so you take what you can get.

The jars were at June's place, stored in boxes in the old stone shed next to the kitchen. I was supposed to bring the daisies that morning and arrange them on the tables in the tent behind the house once the linens and place settings had been laid. I'd picked them the day before, from the field behind my sister's house, which is chock-full of the things. I've never been much a fan of daisies—they've always struck me as bright weeds more than actual flowers. Never mind that they're cheap, but for a wedding, they're not appropriate. Roses and lilies and chrysanthemums, even tulips and lilacs if you're going for something less fancy—but daisies, no.

I remember when the two of them came into the shop. Hands held, dripping with dew. She looked like her mother, but curvier. June has, at least as far as I can remember, more of a boyish figure. And he was just fine, perfectly handsome, I suppose, in the way that nice, clean-cut boys who went to college can be.

They were young. That was the strongest impression they made on me. I didn't think people got married that young anymore. At least not from well-to-do families. Local girls with no plans and knocked up, that's one thing, but a Vassar girl with a job at a magazine in New York and a law student at Columbia, these are not the types of kids you see rushing willy-nilly to the altar. But they certainly were sweet together and had a cloud of luck and love around them that not only stung a little, old, bitter spinster that I am, but surprised me. That kind of affection is not something you see so much around here. Local couples, even the young ones, are worn-out from two jobs, school schedules, family obligations, and too much debt. And the older ones, with their late mortgage payments to make, propane-gas tanks to be filled, and sons and daughters skipping school and smashing cars and getting in fights at the Tap, are too tired, not to mention too busy performing their roles as jolly country folk on the weekends for the pampered and demanding New Yorkers, spending every last drop of civility and patience on these strangers with none left over for their wives and husbands. The weekenders from the city not only take the best houses, views, food, and, yes, flowers our little town has to offer, but they take the best of us, too. They arrive at the end of each week texting and calling from trains and cars with their demands—driveways to be plowed, wood to stack, lawns to mow, gutters needing cleaning, kids to be babysat, groceries to be bought, houses to be cleaned, pillows needing fluffing. For some, we even put up their Christmas trees after Thanksgiving and take them away after New Year's. They never dirty their hands with any of the things the rest of us have to, nor shoulder the actual weight of anything. We can't bear them and yet we are borne by them. It makes for a testy pact that for the most part works. But every once in a while there are some slips. Like when Cindy Showalter, a waitress at the Owl Inn, spat in the face of an old woman who muttered something insulting under her breath when Cindy did not understand the type of cheese the woman was asking for. *Who has ever heard of an Explorer cheese?!?* she asked me at church. I shook my head and later went on the Internet to find a cheese called Explorateur, which I'm sure has never been served in any restaurant around here. There was also the fire that broke out in the barn at Holly Farm and killed three horses. No one ever proved it, but we all know it was Mac Ellis, the former caretaker, who set the place ablaze after being fired by Noreen Schiff for padding the receipts each month. He'd done it for years, apparently, and her accountant in the city finally caught on. He never got arrested but word got out and he lost a few jobs. There's a lot of resentment simmering underneath the smiles and *so good to see you*s and *no problem, happy to do that*s of this town. So when someone crosses the line, it can get uncomfortable.

Many people, the younger girls mostly, felt June Reid had crossed a line when she started up with Luke Morey. They always made a fuss about him. He was good-looking, I'll give you that. Not a surprise since Lydia's father was devil handsome in his day, and Lydia has always been what men seem to find attractive. Even so, much of Luke's looks came from the fact that he didn't look like anyone else around here. He was like a wild orchid growing in a hayfield. No one ever knew who his father was, but they sure knew he was black. I hate to say what it suggests about this town that there is virtually no one who could have been the father. The older couple in Cornwall, dead now, were retired scientists from Boston, and mixed—her black, him white; and the principal's adopted son, Seth, he's black but was only six or seven when Luke was born. This was our town at the time, which no one much thought of to be honest except in instances that exposed it like when Lydia Morey had her baby. It's been at least three decades since that boy was born, but nothing much—at least on that front—has changed. More weekenders, of course, fewer local families, who one by one have sold their farms and land and houses to people who spend maybe a few weeks total in them every year. Saturdays and Sundays, a week or two in the summer. The truth is that most of the houses in this town stand empty. They blink with security gizmos, are scrubbed and dusted and jammed to the ceiling with beautiful furniture, but there's no one home. I drove down South Main Street a few months ago—middle of the week, nine o'clock in the evening after supper at my sister's house—and not a light on anywhere. The moon was out, so I could see the chimney tops and the dormers, but one after the next, all the way down to the town green, dark. It occurred to me that night and since that we no longer live in a town, not a real one anyway. We live in a pricey museum, one that's only open on weekends, and we are its janitors.

It used to be that most of the big, old houses in Wells were owned and lived in by local families. I ought to know because I grew up in one. Granted, it was the rectory at St. David's where my father served as rector for over thirty years, but back then the job came with a six-bedroom house with four fireplaces and a barn down in back. Now there's a rector—some woman called Jesse, if you can believe it—who splits her time between three churches and lives in an apartment in Litchfield. The church rents out the rectory to a young family from the city who come up, yes, you guessed it, on weekends. Of course they have never, not once to my eye anyway, stepped into St. David's. Which is hardly surprising since there are only fifteen or so of us who still come Sunday morning. Like the houses along the green, the old church sits empty save for a handful of hours on weekends. My father retired years ago, and died not long after, but I still go every Sunday. I kept his old key, so I let myself in early and set up the altar flowers with whatever is unsold from the shop and on its way to the garbage. No one can see wilting petals from the pews.

It might shock some of the old-timers at St. David's to find out that I gave up on God a long time ago, when my mother started to disappear into Alzheimer's, which has to be the slowest, cruelest way out there is. She started to go when I was in high school and died a week after my fortieth birthday. By then and for a long time before she was unrecognizable. Angry, awful, and completely dependent on me. My sister went to college and I stayed home to help with what my father was too proud and cheap to hire anyone else to do. Not that I needed one, but it's not exactly easy to find a boyfriend let alone a husband when you're living as an unpaid round-the-clock nurse in your parents' house. I don't waste my time wishing things had gone differently, and I don't pretend that if I'd prayed any harder it would have. I've been on my own without God's help or a husband for a long time now.

Most of the people I grew up with have moved to Torrington or across the state line to Millerton or Amenia, and even those towns are getting expensive. But some manage to burrow into the corners of the town, tuck into its folds, and stay, as I have. Lydia Morey has, too, though it's hard to imagine why. She's the last of her family around here, and by family I don't mean Morey. It's amazing to me she kept that name. She's a Hannafin and she knows it. Who can guess what that woman was ever thinking, so her choice to keep that name is no more of a surprise than her choosing to stick around after she gave birth to that black baby boy. When Luke was born, it was clear to everyone that Lydia's husband, red-headed, freckle-faced Earl Morey, was not the father. He packed Lydia's bags that very night and told her not to come back. She went straight from the maternity ward to her mother's couch. Her mother was still around then, and she took them both in for a while, but she made no secret of her disgust. She worked as a teller at the bank in those days, and you could hear her carrying on at the drive-through to anyone who'd listen about her lunatic daughter, who she was certain had gotten caught up with cults and black men and God knows what. Everyone sided with Earl, who comes from a big family that's been around here forever, and Lydia Morey was for a while as banished as one can be in a town of fifteen hundred people, half of whom barely live here.

Over time, people came around, for the most part. Luke was always liked, especially there for a bit in high school when he was breaking state records for swimming and even, I think, being whispered about for the Olympics; but Lydia remained a loner, save for a few poor choices in the man department. To be fair, the pickings are slim around here, and the poor woman, pretty as she is, did the best she could. With pickings this slim, someone like Luke Morey, once he finally cleaned up his act, became a prize goose at the fair to the women in town. His skin was definitely his father's, whoever that was, but he had his mother's wide-set, green eyes and high cheekbones. Add to that at least six feet and a somewhat successful landscaping business, and you've got enough to turn a few heads. He turned heads his whole life, but never so much as when he went to jail, just a few months after high school, and then, later, when he moved in with June Reid, who was over twenty years his senior and from the city. From the time that boy was born he was the talk of the town, and given what happened, how he went, and how many he took with him, he always will be.

When I drove over to June Reid's that morning with the daisies and saw the nightmare surrounding her property—all that smoke, the old stone house destroyed by fire, the empty tent—I did not stop. I just kept driving. Without thinking, I drove straight to my sister's place, where we sat and drank a pot of mint tea picked fresh from her garden. She'd already been called—by whom I don't know—and she told me what happened. Killed, all of them—the young couple, June's ex-husband, and that doomed Luke Morey. For a long time, we just sat and watched the steam rise from our mother's old, pale green china teacups. Later, I walked out the back door and into the field behind her house. I was out there for hours, unsure what to do or where to go. I wandered through the high grass and all those horrible daisies, from the wood line to the road, back and forth, back and forth, running my old, wrinkled hands over all those bright and unlucky weeds. Eventually, I came in. I stayed the night. And the next night, too.

The daisies did not go to waste. Every single one was put to use. They never did see the inside of any jelly jars, but they found their way into a hundred or more funeral arrangements. Even when no one asked for them—and let's face it, most did not—I still found a way to make them work. No one ever accused me of being a soft touch, but when something like what happened at June Reid's that morning happens, you feel right away like the smallest, weakest person in the world. That nothing you do could possibly matter. That nothing matters. Which is why, when you stumble upon something you can do, you do it. So that's what I did.

Lydia

They arrive before she knows they are there. She has no idea when exactly they settled in at the table by the window, two down from the one where she sits nursing her cold cup of coffee, but it's long enough ago that they have ordered soups and salads and been served their cups of tea. They are behind her, she cannot see them, but by their polite laughter she knows it's tea they are sipping, not coffee; soups and salads they have ordered, not hamburgers and fries, or the meat loaf. She doesn't know these particular women, these mothers and daughters and wives, but she knows them. She has cleaned their houses, ferried their children to train stations and sleepovers, and yanked the weeds from their sidewalks for most of her life. She has heard them fret about global warming, mercury levels in tuna, and pesticides choking the life out of the lettuce they stab with their forks but barely eat. She has witnessed up close their girlish and convincing surprise at the arrival of each relentless windfall and victory. A husband's unexpected bonus at the end of the year, the new station wagon in the driveway strung up with birthday or Christmas or Mother's Day ribbons. What she finds the most difficult to bear is hearing them brag about their children—

the early acceptances to impossible-to-get-into schools, the job offers from prestigious law firms, the promotions and awards, the engagements to attractive people from happy families; their weddings.

It is a wedding they are talking about now. The loud one, the one that begins every sentence with *Now. Now, you'll never believe. Now, Carol, listen to this. Now, I never. Now, can you imagine.* NOW HEAR THIS, she seems to be commanding each time she speaks. As if her voice, two or three decibel levels above the clank and chatter of the restaurant, didn't already demand your attention. She has a daughter getting married in Nantucket. From the shimmy in her voice Lydia can tell it is this woman's favorite thing to talk about. *Thank God for the wedding planner, bossy like you wouldn't believe, but a genius with the details. She even helped organize the honeymoon, a gift from the groom's parents. A month in Asia. To be honest, I think it's too much—the whole thing waiting like a giant game-show prize on the other side of what we expect to be a perfectly nice but by no means over-the-top wedding. They're from New Jersey,* she explains. *Big Italian family,* she adds, and just in case anyone missed the point: *They don't know any better.*

She keeps going. *The trip is endless.* Her voice is a furrowed brow, bragging. *India, Vietnam, Thailand,* each country's name rolling off her tongue like the brand names of pricey clothing Lydia sees ads for in the thick beauty magazines these women drop on the bathroom floor like just-once-used towels.

As she continues on about the groom's family— the limousine service they've owned since the 1950s, their accents, their Catholicism—Lydia looks out the window to the only motel in town, the Betsy. The sign is large and wooden and covered in white paint that has been cracked and peeling for as long as she's lived here, which is always. The sign has a large pediment on top as if announcing a grand colonial inn and not the twenty-one-room, one-story, white-brick motel that sits out of sight, beyond the tree line, at the end of the drive. Nothing is grand about the Betsy except maybe the room numbers painted in robin's-egg blue with gold borders on the small oval plaques hanging from each door. The owner's mother fancied herself a folk artist, and they were a gift to her son Tommy when he opened the motel in the late sixties. He told Lydia the story one night at the Tap, a few years after he sold the place. Lydia had cleaned the rooms there for six or seven years before the new owners came in and hired Mexicans, who arrive on foot each morning from across the state line in Amenia or Millerton. She'd never said much to Tommy when she worked for him, nor he to her, but since time had passed and they were both bellied up to the same bar, he got chatty. *I hated that color blue,* he spat, many drinks in and looking like a sixty-five-year-old teenager—gray hair, liver spots, cracking voice, bright blue eyes, lost. Wearing the same white, button-down shirt and khaki pants she remembered him wearing in church when she was a kid. *She covered everything in that blue and insisted I put her silly paintings in the rooms. She even painted flowers on some of the beds. I named the place after her thinking it would open her purse a bit more, but it didn't. I was supposed to live off the earnings but there never were any. No one comes to Wells to stay in a motel.*

Everyone in town knew Betsy Ball had, long ago, married the heir to a liquor fortune who died young and left her everything. Tommy lived with his mother most of his life, sleeping in the same bedroom he slept in as a child, in the house he still lived in. Lydia wondered if he ever left that room, ever moved to another one in a different part of that big brick house on South Main Street after his mother died. Except for four years in Pennsylvania for college, and a few years after in the city, Tommy Ball never really left town. Never dated anyone that anyone can remember and never married. Betsy Ball saw Tommy every day and he hated her, Lydia thought. Her son hated her but she was not alone. Even when the town library, to which she eventually left a good deal of money, threw her a party for her one hundredth birthday, her son arrived and left with her. She was widowed and deaf, probably wearing diapers and not knowing her own name, but she did not go home alone that night.

Alone and home is where Lydia has been the most during the last six months since Luke died. She walks to the coffee shop after lunch most days to get a break from the television, which has become like a full-time job. If the morning talk shows start without her, she feels like she's dropping the ball, as if she's failed in the one measly duty she has each day. There aren't as many of the old-time Phil Donahue–type shows anymore, the kind with regular people with extraordinary problems. Now the shows are more specific: medical, food-focused, or exclusively dedicated to celebrities, who at times feel like family—like cousins you hear about in Christmas letters doing this and that, who you catch glimpses of at graduation parties, christenings, or weddings. It comforts Lydia to see the same people pop up on the same couches and guest chairs through the years. They age, she ages, the talk-show hosts age. For a little while it seems like they are all in it together.

Now, did you know the caterer never got paid? At first, she thinks the loud one is still talking about her daughter's wedding in Nantucket, but she's moved on to the past tense, another subject, a different wedding. It is soon clear which one.

Lydia scans the place for the waitress, the pregnant blonde named Amy, who she's pretty sure used to work at the grocery store. She sees her each day and keeps meaning to ask, but after she orders her coffee she can't ever seem to find the words. Lately, Amy just brings the coffee, which excuses both of them from speaking.

The lunch crowd has mostly left. Lydia pivots back, slightly, careful not to turn all the way around and be seen by the loud one or any of the women with her. She still doesn't know quite who they are, but given what they are now talking about, she doesn't want to be recognized. She wants to leave as quickly and quietly as possible. She looks again toward the kitchen, hoping to see Amy and signal for the check, but there is no one. She's stuck and there is nothing she can do to keep from hearing this woman, who seems to not take even the shortest breath between her words.

I don't think the tent was burned. But the big oak tree behind the house caught fire. They still haven't cut down what's left. It stands there, black and horrible, like some scary Halloween decoration. Now, can you imagine?

My brother used to work for Luke Morey. . . . Someone else is speaking now, someone younger. *He was at the house the day before it happened, with his friends—mowing the lawn, picking up sticks, weeding the flower beds. . . . Silas still won't talk about it. He's only fifteen. The police asked him questions, the fire marshal, too, but he didn't know anything. He worked for Luke for three summers.*

Lydia thought this kind of talk had died down. And even if it hadn't, she wasn't usually within earshot to hear it. Most people, if they saw her coming, changed the subject or got quiet. She'd become used to conversations ending abruptly and eyes looking away from her as she passed people in the pharmacy and the grocery store, or even here at the coffee shop. But these women don't see her.

Amy must be resting—the lunch rush looked like it had been busy, and she's at least five months along. Lydia remembers cleaning houses until her ninth month and going back to work with Luke when he was only two weeks old. She had to. Earl had thrown her out without a penny, and no one blamed him. Luke's biological father didn't know he existed, nor would he ever, and her mother had been barely scraping by on what she made at the bank. Lydia and her mother had been on their own for as long as she could remember. Her father died of a heart attack soon after she was born, and all he left behind was debt. An outstanding loan with the bank and payments on the truck he used to plow driveways with in the winter to make money. *There is no pension plan when you sell firewood and plow snow for a living,* Lydia's mother would say when she was paying bills and smoking cigarettes at the table in her kitchen. *He worked hard* was half of the only other comment she'd make about Patrick Hannafin, who was, from the few photographs Lydia had seen, the source of her dark brown hair and high, sharp cheekbones. In every photograph he looked the same: handsome, tall, serious. *He worked hard,* Natalie Hannafin would say of her late husband, *but his hands were allergic to money.* His family had been in Wells since the 1800s, and at one time there had been as many of them as Moreys, but over the years, sickness and wanderlust and more baby girls born than boys dwindled the fold, and now Lydia was the last Hannafin standing.

Still, Lydia's mother insisted she keep Earl Morey's name after the divorce and that Luke keep it, too. It made no sense, and what was worse was that it seemed like an aggressive stance to take against a family who not only took their name seriously but didn't take any more kindly to an open challenge than they did infidelity. Lydia knew her mother held out some tissue-thin hope that Earl would change his mind, forgive her daughter, and take Lydia and Luke back. Retaining that name was her one demand at the time, and because her apartment was the only place Lydia could go after the hospital, she agreed. Lydia slept on her mother's couch for six months, and since there was no money for a sitter, Lydia would bring Luke with her to the Betsy and into the houses she cleaned, still in his car seat, setting him on kitchen counters, window seats, and beds while she worked. Her mother always said the boy could sleep through a war.

The loud one is at it again, filling everyone in on the details. The same grim facts the papers and the New York and Connecticut news stations repeated for months. A gas leak, an explosion, four people dead, a young couple to be married later that day, the mother of the bride standing on the lawn watching it happen, her ex-husband asleep upstairs and her boyfriend in the kitchen, *an ex-con,* she makes sure to emphasize, *and black, not that it matters,* she adds in a whisper.

My God, she can hear one of them say quietly. *What a nightmare,* she hears another mumble with what Lydia imagines is a slowly shaking head and crossed arms.

Finally, the fourth woman speaks. She must be the only one not from around here, Lydia thinks, and it must be for her benefit that these women are so painstakingly reporting the story. *How do you recover from that? How would you even begin?*

Lydia puts both hands in her lap and closes her eyes as the loud one winds up.

You don't, that's how, and she didn't. Now can you imagine watching everyone you love just disappear? Have you ever even heard of such a thing?

There's nothing she can do to stop them. Nothing she can do to shut them up or shut them down. They are like the horseflies that circle her head when she walks along the town green in the summer. They dart and poke and buzz and dive, keeping pace no matter how slowly or quickly she moves.

She's left town, apparently. West, or south, or something. After the funerals she just vanished.

For a few long seconds there is silence. The clang of lunch dishes being washed and stacked in the kitchen. The gentle beeping sound of a delivery truck backing up, somewhere.

There was an investigation, says the woman who does not sound at all familiar but who must be from Wells or nearby to assume the role of storyteller. *There's no hard proof but it looks like it was that black boy she was seeing. And forgive me, he was a boy and on the one hand good for her, but look what happened.*

Do you really think it was his fault? the younger one asks nervously. Since she spoke about her brother earlier, she has remained silent. *Silas says Luke was a good boss. Our mother disagrees but Silas liked him.*

Now . . . c'mon . . . I don't think anyone really doubts that it was his doing. He was the one in the kitchen. Everyone else was asleep. And besides, he'd been in prison. For using drugs,

43

dealing, the whole shebang. Cocaine or crack or methamphetamines or something. They were quite a pair. She ran art galleries in the city and I think she moved up here full-time. To be with him, no doubt.

How would a woman like that end up with a local thug like him anyway? the fourth one asks, as if on cue.

How do you think?

NOW HEAR THIS, Lydia has shouted, the words not even hers. She is standing, her chair scraping like a scream as she rises, turning to face these women. *NOW,* she shouts again, her voice a shock to her ears, the loudest sound she has made in many months. When was the last time she even spoke? Yesterday? Last week? She is standing in front of these four women, three of them near her age, midfifties, early sixties, and one of them much younger, in her twenties, the only one she recognizes. Her name is Holly, and Lydia grew up with her mother, who was a few years older and never friendly. Seconds pass as she stands in this now-almost-empty coffee shop before a table of women, who, besides Holly, she imagines have not once worked a day of physical labor, who have been attended by loving parents and friends and colleagues and boyfriends and husbands and children and grandchildren every pampered, taken-for-granted minute of their lives. These are comfortable women, cherished women. They

44

look at her as if the forks in their hands have told them to be quiet.

I'm sorry, who are you? The loud one, attempting to impose order, breaks the silence and deflates Lydia's momentary authority. Who am I? Lydia thinks. I'm nothing. I've never been anyone except someone's housekeeper, daughter, wife, girlfriend, or mother, and in all of those roles I have failed and now I play no role. Her knees are twitching and she can smell her sharp body odor. She is standing before these women with nothing to say beyond the demand that they listen. Holly begins to speak: *Lydia . . . I mean . . . Mrs. Morey, I'm so . . .*

As she speaks her name, Lydia's face flashes with heat, and a panic that registers as physical pain knuckles through her chest. Before another word is spoken, she turns away, shakily places a sweaty five-dollar bill on the table, and, as she does, mumbles, *That thug is my son.*

Excuse me, what did you say? the loud one asks, her voice high, tight, scolding more than curious.

Lydia turns to face her. *My son, you stupid bitch. He is . . . He was my son.* She steps toward her as she says the words, and when she sees the woman flinch, she realizes that her hand is raised, her palm open. She stops abruptly and hurries as quickly and as steadily as she can manage toward the door, out across the shopping-center parking lot, and onto the sidewalk that leads home.

She has heard, finally, what she feared people believed. It took more than six months for the words to reach her ears, and now that they have, she needs to get as far away from them as she can. She has no one to call, no one to rush home to. But when has she? She reviews the few possibilities—Earl; her mother; her father, who died before she knew him; Luke's father, for only a little while; Rex, for too long, for which she will never forgive herself; Luke; June. None of these people were ever hers. They either belonged to someone else or had lives or lies that put them out of reach, or should have. This is not news, but what surprises her, after being alone for so long, is that it's only now that it feels unbearable.

The sidewalk that leads to town is slick with leaves. They turned color late this year, some as late as Halloween, and clung to their branches until a nor'easter blew in and finally knocked them to earth. They are everywhere. She wants to run, but instead walks slowly, careful not to slip and cause another scene as she passes in front of the auto shop, the hospital thrift store, the flower shop, the historical society, the fabric store, the town library, the elementary school.

Each day, even in the rain, she walks. Her car, an old, light blue Chevy Lumina, parked behind the apartment building where she lives, hasn't been driven in over a month. She only ever used it for cleaning jobs, and if she needed to go somewhere in town, she always saved gas by walking. The grocery store and the coffee shop are her only destinations now and she goes to both on foot.

She walks past St. David's, where Luke's funeral was held, the same church her mother took her to on Christmas Eves and Easter Sundays when she was growing up. *Whether God is or isn't, we cover the base,* is what she'd say. And for that reason insisted she and Earl get married there, too. Luke's funeral was the first time Lydia had stepped foot in the place since her wedding day and it surprised her that nothing had changed in over thirty years. The same dark wood, the same gloomy stained glass. *God isn't,* she whispered that day, to herself and to her dead mother. And if He was, Lydia knew He'd long ago looked past her.

She walks past the small house she grew up in next to the firehouse, the two-family Victorian where she lived when she was married, briefly; the apartment above Bart Pitcher's garage, where her mother lived the last fifteen years of her life; the apartment three streets away, behind the liquor store, where she went to live after her divorce was final and where she raised Luke. She should have left this town by now, she thinks, ducking under a low-hanging branch. There is no one here, but there is no one anywhere. For a while there was, when Luke was young and it was just the two of them. But as he grew older, he found swimming and friends and started to occupy a world apart from her, even though they lived under the same roof. Then much later, after prison and years of avoiding her, he came back, and only because June made him. That began a brief time, so anomalous and happy, she remembers it now as if she'd made it up. Like a fable in which some wretch is given a glimpse of paradise only to have it snatched away. She is that wretch. Luke, letting her back in his life, and with him, June: so much more than she had expected. And now both of them, in a puff of black smoke, gone.

She kicks at a pile of leaves that have been raked and left uncollected on the sidewalk and considers the thousands of times she's walked here—as a little kid, a teenager, a mother, and now. She can't imagine anyone walking these sidewalks as many times as she has. My feet are famous to these sidewalks, she thinks, and the idea almost amuses her, its novelty breaking for a split second the panic that drove her from the coffee shop. She holds her breath as she walks past the cemetery—perhaps the only childhood superstition she still holds on to. She clears the street corner that marks the end of the property and exhales, imagining all the thwarted ghosts—including her parents—who wait inside the cemetery gates for her to join them. Luke is buried in the small cemetery behind St. John's Church, where Lolly Reid was supposed to be married. It's across the road from where June's house had been and seemed to Lydia the obvious place. In addition to Luke's plot, she bought two more— one for her and, though she never had the chance to tell her, one for June.

As she crosses the street and rejoins the sidewalk, she has a sharp sense that someone is behind her. She thinks she hears footsteps, but when she stops and turns around, no one is there, just a teenager riding his bike on the street, heading in the opposite direction. *The ghosts are out today,* Lydia remembers her mother saying on dark winter days like this. She starts walking again, faster now, and remembers how Luke once called her a ghost. He didn't say it kindly and it was before he began to forgive her, before June. He was standing in the section of the grocery store where the ice cream and frozen pizzas are displayed in clear-doored freezers. She had seen him enter the store and followed him in, kept a distance as she watched him move from aisle to aisle and fill his cart. He'd been out of prison for an entire summer and she'd still not spoken to him, even though she'd left him many unanswered notes and phone messages. His shirt was too small and it rode up his back as he bent to lift a bag of ice. She could see the thick cord of his spine and the muscles on either side wriggling like snakes under his dark skin. How on earth could I have created something so beautiful? she thought. When he saw her, he stood still and stared for several seconds, and then began to turn away. But before he did, he stopped abruptly and spat, *Go away, ghost.*

She crosses the village green toward the small apartment building where she has lived on the first floor for more than six years. She climbs the rickety porch steps and notices she left a lamp on in the living room. She figures a moth of some kind must be banging against the bulb, because the light dances and casts small, fast shadows across the couch, the chair, the wall. She pauses at the door and lets herself see for a moment what she imagines most people come home to—lit rooms, voices, someone waiting.

It is raining now. Somewhere on Upper Main Street a metal mailbox slams shut. She thinks she hears footsteps again, this time rushing away, but soon there is only the sound of raindrops tapping the fallen leaves, the parked cars, the gutters. She closes her eyes and listens. No one calls her name, there are no more footsteps behind her, but still she turns around before unlocking the door and stepping inside. She takes a long, late-day look at the town where she has lived her whole life, where there are no friends, no family, but where her feet are famous to the sidewalks.

Rick

My mom made Lolly Reid's wedding cake. She got the recipe from a Brazilian restaurant in the city where she went one night after going in with her friends to see a show. It was a coconut cake made with fresh oranges. She prepared for days. It didn't have any pillars or platforms or fancy decorations; just a big sheet cake with a scattering of those tiny, silver edible balls and a few purple orchids she had special-ordered from Edith Tobin's shop. She was proud of that cake. She bakes and decorates cakes for all the birthdays in our family, and she made the wedding cake for my sister's wedding, and mine; so when June Reid hired us to cater her daughter Lolly's wedding, I thought, Why not?

Unfortunately, she never got paid. I didn't either. Not a cent. And if June Reid had tried to pay me, I would have torn up the check. I couldn't accept money from that woman after what she'd been through. My wife, Sandy, saw it differently, still does, but that's her business and this is mine. We own Feast of Reason together, and technically she has a right to complain, but I wasn't—and am still not—about to pester June Reid for a few dollars. Twenty-two thousand dollars to be exact, but who's counting? I should have worked up a contract like Sandy was always on me to do—at least we would have had half the money up front—but I never got around to drafting one and running it by a lawyer to make sure it covered all the bases. Lolly Reid's wedding was only the second big event we'd been hired to cater, and we were still getting the farm market and café on its feet, making sure everything there was up to code. If you want to lose sleep at night and eliminate all your free time or freedom, by all means open a small business, especially one that serves food. No one tells you about health inspectors or wheel-chair access when you're first thinking of opening a place that serves the perfect lentil soup, fresh-baked bread, and almond-milk cappuccino. And it's a good thing they don't, because otherwise there would be no restaurants or cafés or coffee shops anywhere. I'm not sure why we thought the catering bit was a good idea, but it gives people you like a way to make some cash. Also, it's flattering to be asked to make the food for someone's important day—wedding or graduation or birthday. And when it's someone like June Reid, who could've had anyone from the city come up and do a first-class job, well, for us, it was a big deal. When she and Lolly came in and asked me if we'd be interested in making the food for the wedding, there was no way we were going to say no. June Reid would have been a hard woman to say no to anyway; she had that Glinda the Good Witch vibe to her, a sort of nothing-bad-has-ever-happened-to-me-and-nothing-bad-will-happen-to-you-if-you're-around-me feel. She was pretty in the way that some of the older women on my wife's soap operas are pretty. She took care of herself. She smelled good, too, like I don't know what but *nice*. I guess she probably still does, but we haven't seen her around here in a while. She took off months ago, and who can blame her? She pulled herself together for the funerals, kept her distance from everyone in town, and then was gone.

June Reid had been coming to Wells on the weekends with her husband and daughter for years and then, later, on her own, when she moved here full-time. No one ever made a fuss or thought twice about her, but when she shacked up with Luke Morey the whole town paid attention. This was more than a couple of years ago, and at the time she must have been at least fifty, about twice Luke's age. Sandy and her friends never got tired of talking about it. They just couldn't accept that he would hitch his horse to her wagon, or however the phrase goes, especially since Luke had more than plenty of wagons to choose from. We grew up together, went to the same elementary and high school, played on a lot of the same sports teams, too, until high school, when he dedicated every free second he could to swimming. And Jesus could he swim. Perry Lynch used to joke that it's because his people were from Cuba or Puerto Rico and came to this country by swimming to Florida, but like with most things, Perry got it wrong. Luke's mom, Lydia, was white, but his dad, whoever he was, must have been straight-up black and not Hispanic or Latino or whatever you call it. In any case, Luke swam like a fish and broke school and state records and even got recruited by a few big universities— including Stanford—for scholarships. Stanford! He had the touch and had his pick of girls, schools, and futures. But then it all fell apart. All at once—bam—he was just like the rest of us, worse even. He got snagged for moving coke from Connecticut to Kingston and his whole life collapsed. He ended up serving eleven months in a prison in Adirondack, New York. It was unbelievable, and the shittiest part was that whole thing was rigged. Everybody knew Luke had nothing to do with drugs in high school. He was always too focused on swimming and keeping in shape. He drank like the rest of us on weekends. He even passed out once on the town green coming back from a party when we were sophomores. Strange to think how much of a big deal that was back then. Everyone knew about it and someone must have called Gus, the town cop, because he was the one to come down, wake him up, and walk him home.

Luke wasn't perfect, but for him to get caught

with a major cocaine haul made no sense. It still doesn't. I'd heard that his mother, Lydia, somehow had something to do with it, one of her shady boyfriends. And later I was told by a guy who works in the Beacon Police Department that Luke had been screwed into pleading guilty by a lawyer and a crooked judge who were protecting bigger fish. Whatever went down, Luke never said anything about it to me or anyone else I know. After he got out, he came back to Wells, got jobs here and there, and eventually started his landscaping business. One thing about Luke is that he never talked shit about other people. He could be moody and sometimes lose his temper, but he didn't talk trash. That his mother had been gossiped about so much over the years must have had something to do with it. Who knows. Even when he'd start seeing some girl, it was always from somebody else that I'd find out. Growing up, the rest of us practically took out ads in the paper when we got to first, second, and third base. And home run, Jesus, everyone had to know and usually within a few hours. But not Luke. He played it cool. Like when he started up with June Reid. Sandy's the one who told me—she keeps tabs on everyone—and by the time I found out, he was already living in that old stone house on Indian Pond Road. I must have seen him once or twice a week back then and he never mentioned it.

When Luke first got out of prison, his swimming

coach from high school, Mr. Delinsky, got him a job lifeguarding at the town beach. I was down there all the time with Sandy and Liam, who was just an infant. It was before we started Feast of Reason and I was still working evenings, mostly on the weekends, for a catering company in Cornwall. My days were free and we were living with my mother, so we would park Liam on a towel at the lake and kick back. Luke was there, and Jesus if he didn't get big in prison. He's always kept his shit tight, but with swimming the guys never get too bulky. He must have lifted weights every day, because it looked like he'd put on at least twenty pounds of muscle. He was ripped. He'd be up on that white chair looking out over the kids splashing around in the algae-covered lake, black as a berry and built like an Olympian. It's a weird thing to say, but he was like a movie star or a famous athlete. Too big, too handsome, too *something* for the likes of us. No one around here looked like he did, and I don't just mean because he was black. I caught Sandy looking at him more than a few times, and I thought what the heck, who can blame her?

He worked as a lifeguard for most of that summer. By August, a few of the mothers who took their kids to the lake complained about the town hiring someone fresh out of jail and he had to give up the job. After that he started helping out with Steve Pitcher's estate management company.

Raking leaves, cleaning gutters, clearing brush. He did that for a couple summers, and in the evenings and in the winter I got him a few cater-waiter jobs for big events at Harkness. The company I worked for had a contract with the boarding school for their fancier alumni events and we always needed help. I'd watch Luke move through the room fetching coffee and pouring wine for these white-haired, old bankers and lawyers in blue blazers and think there was something very wrong. At that point he would have been a sophomore at Stanford, winning races, planning a future filled with nights like this, but with him being waited on and not the other way around. It's not that I think one life is better than the other—hell, I'll be serving white-haired New Yorkers in blue blazers the rest of my life—but it's just that this wasn't the life he was *supposed* to live. Anyone who knew Luke in high school could tell he was not long for our town. Of all the lazy potheads and drunks we grew up with, who one way or another have managed to live off disability checks, insurance settlements, or both, who would ever have guessed that it would be Luke Morey who would be buried here at thirty years old? No one, that's who. Not even Dirk Morey or his old man, Earl, who used to be married to Luke's mom. Those crazy, redheaded Moreys never liked Luke—and fair enough, they had their reasons—but the truth is that Luke never did anything to them besides being born and having the same name. It didn't matter. He was always in their crosshairs, and in a town as small as Wells you're bound to cross paths with everyone, even the people you want to avoid. And despite the fact that Dirk was a little guy and a few years younger than us, he was always just over our shoulders cracking jokes, giving Luke a rough time. Luke could take care of himself, but there were a few times some of us had to step in. Dirk's the only person I've ever punched, and the night I did, he had it coming. It'd be one thing if we were still kids, but this was only a few years ago. We were leaving the elementary-school cafeteria, where the volunteer fire department has its monthly spaghetti dinners. Everyone goes. They always have. June and Luke had already walked out, and Dirk was behind me and Sandy. *Looks like he found a broad just like his mother,* he said, poking his finger into my back and looking up ahead at Luke and June. I ignored Dirk as most of us do when he's had a few too many beers. Usually he'll shut the fuck up and move on, but not that night. *Some of 'em just like dark meat, I guess. Funny thing, eh, Rick?* He poked my back again and I could feel my fists clench. Luke and June were only a few yards ahead of us, but I don't think they could hear. And then, making sure everyone in the cafeteria could hear: *Difference is this rich cunt pays for it.* With that, I spun around and decked him. Half the town at one time or another has wanted to deck Dirk Morey, and some of them have. He's been hauled out of the Tap almost as many times as his father. The Moreys are loud drunks, but they're little guys, wiry, and as aggressive as they can get, they usually avoid a brawl. Problem is that there are so many of them around here. Dirk always feels free to mouth off because there are usually two or three cousins nearby to defend him if he gets in a scrape. His family *is* the volunteer fire department, so he must have felt bigger than usual that night. It was lucky that Luke got to me before any Moreys did, because after I hit Dirk the first time, I shoved him to the floor and dove in. I'd heard this guy heckle and mouth off since we were kids, and I'd saved up a few swipes over the years. I got a couple good ones in, too, before Luke dragged me off to the parking lot. June Reid stood to the side while Luke made sure I wasn't going back in for more, but when Sandy and I started walking to our car, June ran up and grabbed my hand. Not a thank-you, no words. She pulled one of my hands into hers, squeezed it, and let go. She was looking down the whole time, so I couldn't see if there were tears on her face, but she was upset. She rushed back to Luke before I could say anything.

I didn't know much about June Reid before she starting seeing Luke. I knew the house—it was one of the oldest in Wells, and I remember going there as a kid at Halloween for candy and being frightened because the place looked haunted. It's funny to imagine that she would have been roughly my age now when I came knocking at her door in my He-Man costume. When I first heard about her with Luke, I thought it was a little weird, but when I saw them together, I was mostly glad to see Luke lighten up, begin to have fun again. He was a pretty depressed guy when he came out of prison. And he didn't hang out much. He crashed in a room above Mr. Delinsky's garage for those first few months and then got an apartment near the hospital. I'd see him at the lake and then at Harkness, but besides that he kept to himself, went to the gym at the high school and still swam laps in the pool. I saw him there with June a few times, working out. I think it was the first time I heard him laughing or saw him smiling since high school. I remember one time watching him attempt to teach her a complicated exercise with free weights and was surprised to see how quickly he got frustrated by how uncoordinated she was. She didn't seem to mind and instead teased him by mimicking his serious face and exaggerating his careful movements. He was clearly annoyed but she was relentless and eventually he couldn't help but smile. I don't think most people would have expected June Reid to have a silly side, but she did, and I think it was just one of a number of things about her that brought Luke back to life.

When my mother found out what happened, she asked me to bring the cake down to the firehouse for the guys who'd been called out to June's place that morning. Dirk Morey was there when I arrived and so was Earl, along with all the others. For once these guys had nothing to say. I brought the cake into the kitchen and told Dirk's cousin Eddie that I'd come back next week for the tray. I got out of there as fast as I could. I didn't want to hear any of the grisly details. I just wanted to get home to Sandy and Liam and lock the door. I started back to our place, but for the first time since my dad died when I was in eighth grade, I started to cry. Maybe it was because both were accidents—my dad's car got hit head-on by a drunk driver on Route 22 after he picked up some part for Mom's dishwasher. Or maybe it was because Luke had become a friend. We were always friendly growing up, but he had his eyes elsewhere—girls, swimming, college—and for better or for worse we never were that tight. But after he got out of jail and was up and running with his landscaping business, we saw each other all the time. He'd swing by with the Waller boys for a cup of coffee and a pastry in the mornings while we were opening up. We never got too deep into anything, never talked about his arrest or his time in jail or the life he missed out on, but I knew he and his mom were patching things up after a lot of years of not speaking. He never said

61

a word about it to me, but Sandy knew that June had brokered some kind of truce. When you see someone every day for a while, you settle into a rhythm and you come to count on them even if for nothing more than the fifteen minutes each morning they spend sitting at your counter, on one of your stools, talking about the weather and giving you a big smile and thumbs-up when they sink their teeth into a poppy-seed muffin. I never talked to Luke about my dad or Sandy or Liam, our money troubles, or my mother's second breast-cancer scare last year. I don't talk about that stuff with anyone but Sandy.

People say Luke was responsible for what happened. That June was dumping him and he wanted to get back at her or that he was high that night and accidently left the gas going. For a while a hateful rumor went around that one of the Moreys from the volunteer fire department found a crack pipe in the kitchen near Luke's body. Sure they did. But facts never got in anyone's way when it came to Luke, so I guess it should be no surprise that the story of what happened that night would be no different. What might have cleared things up would have been a proper investigation, but for reasons that no one can explain, what was left of the house was bulldozed and destroyed before the state could examine the wreckage properly and locate the exact cause of the explosion. The county fire chief told me when I called to ask what the hell was going on that they *cleared the site* for safety reasons, to prevent accidents; but given that June Reid had no neighbors besides the Moonies and the Episcopal church down the road, my guess is that it was the town protecting itself from liability. Thoughtless fuckers. One more time the system failed Luke Morey and trampled the facts to serve itself. Funny how no one seemed to mind. June Reid vanished, Lydia Morey quit her housecleaning jobs and now keeps to herself, and the family of the guy who was going to marry Lolly left right after the funerals and went home to California or Washington State, somewhere on the West Coast. There was no one left to push for the truth, and everyone else didn't care. What use was the truth when they had Luke, the ex-con, bastard black son of the town floozy who landed in a pot of honey with an older gal from the city. *It follows a logic,* one of my customers said at the time. He's an old-timer who comes in every morning for a grilled cheese with egg and coffee and he's not a bad guy, just an old man who never left this town and never will. I let him finish his toast and sip his coffee and I didn't say a word.

June Reid didn't stick around long enough to clear up any of these stories. I used to get worked up about it and sometimes I guess I still can, but I've learned that people will believe what they believe no matter what you say or do. What I know about Luke is that he was a friend of mine. He was a good man who had come through some hard times who got to be happy for a little while. And now he's gone.

I didn't want Sandy and Liam to see me blubbering that day, so after I dropped the cake off at the firehouse, I drove to my mother's place. She still lives in the same house I grew up in, the same place where Sandy and I lived when we were trying to get on our feet. Funny how in a small town like ours things play out, circle back, end up. Who would have thought that one day Earl Morey, with his son Dirk, and all their brothers and cousins, would be eating Brazilian wedding cake made by my mother and meant for the daughter of Luke Morey's older, city-rich girlfriend? No one, that's who. But the crazy, haphazard upside down of it all somehow made sense.

I sat in my childhood driveway and watched my mother turn on the porch light, something she always does before opening the front door, since I was a kid and even in broad daylight. I watched her shut the door behind her and pull her thin housecoat tight around her bony shoulders and button the top two buttons. I thought of her squeezing all those damned oranges and cracking all those coconuts for the last two days, sprinkling the little silver balls that the Moreys were now crunching in their tobacco-stained teeth down at the firehouse. And then I started to laugh. I couldn't help it. Nothing was funny, not one thing, but it was all so absurd and fucked-up. Tears and snot were everywhere, and here was my mother, making her way from the stoop to the driveway, shuffling in her slippers, old. She'd left her glasses in the house and I could see her squinting to see me more clearly. *Rick? You okay?* she asked as she stepped to my side of the car and tapped the window. This was my mother: both hands on the roof of the car, leaning into the window, half-blind, worried. Funny how disasters can make you see what you could lose. I don't think I'd ever seen my mother as clearly as I did that day: sixty-six, widowed at fifty, a secretary at the elementary school for over thirty-five years; a single mom who raised two kids, who took care of her grand-daughter while my divorced sister went to nursing school in Hartford; a breast-cancer survivor who let her grown son move back in with his nineteen-year-old wife and one-year-old boy.

You okay in there? she asked, tapping the window again. *Rick?* I unlocked the door and got out of the car. It was now evening. *Tell me,* she said, her hands on my shoulders, her feet balancing on tippy-toes. I leaned in and put my arms around her little body. *It was a good cake, Mom* was all I could think to say. *They would have loved it.*

Rebecca

Some days she doesn't come out. Some days you never see so much as a flicker of light behind the curtains. We've gotten used to her and it's convenient that she pays cash for the room. She leaves a forty-dollar tip each week for Cissy, too, which has to be a record here at the Moonstone. Cissy, like us, is in her early fifties, maybe a bit older. She walks to work from her house down the road, brings our mystery guest a thermos most days and occasionally cookies, and spends nearly an hour cleaning her room when she barely spends twenty minutes in the others. She also, I have seen recently, takes away a small bag of laundry each week from Room 6 and returns it the next day, presumably washed and folded.

Why this woman would want to stay here as long as she has is not our business, but of course I wonder. When she checked in, she had no ID. She'd lost her driver's license, she explained, and then asked if she could pay cash, a month in advance. I called Kelly, who is a better judge of character than I am, to come over from the house before agreeing. She asked the woman how long she planned to stay, and she answered that she didn't know but she would pay each month up front in cash and wouldn't expect a refund if she left early. Kelly asked her where she was from, and even though she answered vaguely, *Back East,* Kelly still turned to me, gave me a wink and a squeeze on my arm, and said to the woman, *Stay here as long as you like.* If she were some rough type or strung-out junkie, there's no way we'd go along with it, but this woman could be anyone's mom or wife and seemed, and still seems, only sad, not dangerous. The night she checked in, I asked her what we should call her, and she said Jane, which of course can't be her real name. But even saying that one word, that fake name, seemed like an effort, and I immediately regretted asking. I walked her out to Room 6—the one closest to and facing the ocean—because she'd asked for it specifically. She must have known someone who'd stayed at the Moonstone once or been here before we owned it. Room 6 also has the best mattress, which we had to buy last year after an older man who'd come down from Seattle for the weekend fell asleep with a lit cigarette in his hand and caught the bed on fire. Burned a hole right through to the other side in the short time it took for him to wake up from the smoke, thank God, and come running to our door in his bare feet and boxer shorts. Which is all to say, since she's staying for as long as she is, I'm glad she's at least sleeping on a decent mattress.

When I showed her to the room, I offered to give her a little tour, but she politely declined. She simply unlocked the door with the key, went in without another word, and stayed inside for nearly a week. It was Cissy who got her out of there the first time. *Ma'am, MA'AM!* she yelled as she knocked. *Out you go, ma'am. Out. I only need a few minutes but you gotta get out.* Kelly and I stood a few doors down to see what would happen. Few people stand up to Cissy. She is tall and thin and strong with one long braid, once black and now silver, thick as rope, down her back. Her hands are bigger than most men's and her chest is as flat as a board. She looks like a Native American, but when I asked her once, she didn't answer. Her husband was from a long line of fishermen in Aberdeen, just down at the mouth of Grays Harbor, but he died of lung cancer fifteen years ago and since then she's been living with her sisters, who I think mostly all lost their husbands one way or another and ended up back in the house they grew up in. Cissy has lived here in Moclips all her life and has worked at the Moonstone since her husband died. According to her sister Pam, Cissy's husband left her the house they'd lived in together, which she sold, so I don't think it's the money Cissy is after so much as something to do and somewhere to go each day. Pam is the only real estate agent in Moclips and the one who sold us the Moonstone from an old couple who'd had it since the sixties. That was four years ago. The first morning in our little house next to the Moonstone, Cissy showed up with a blue tin of orange drop cookies and told us what she charged, what time of the day she worked, and the week in July she took off every year. I don't remember us offering her the job so much as agreeing to her terms. We didn't find out she was Pam's sister for months.

Cissy isn't much for hanging around and gabbing. At first we thought it was because she felt uncomfortable with us because of the gay thing, but when gay marriage was legalized in Washington State this year, she came into the office the morning after the election and said, *It's none of my business, but if you two decide to get legal, I happen to be an ordained minister thanks to the good old Internet and I'd be happy to do the honors.* Kelly is hardly ever at a loss for words, but it did take her a few beats to say thank you and let her know we weren't sure whether we would or wouldn't, and if we did, we'd likely call on her services. Funny how you think people are one way or the other and most of the time you end up completely wrong. We're still not sure about getting married. We've talked about it, of course, and we cheered the night of the election when we saw on television that voters passed the referendum. But beyond Kelly's brothers and nephews, who we see once or twice a year, neither of us have much by way of family anymore. And we've been together for so long now—twenty years, twenty-one, it's hard to remember—it seems like something to let the young ones get excited about. But you never know.

Cissy has never once mentioned her husband, whose name we know was Ben only because Pam told us one night when we cooked her supper. She'd had a few glasses of wine and had been loud and laughing until the subject turned to Cissy, when she quieted to a whisper as if Cissy could hear from their house down the road. *They met at a bar in Aberdeen one night when they were both teenagers. Ben was the only man tall enough for Cissy is what most people thought at the time—and even though you'd never hear them say much to each other, there was a spark between them, always, a kind of animal energy. Cissy used to say I have my sisters for talking and Ben for everything else. They never had kids. Neither of them ever went to a doctor to find out why. They just accepted it and went about their lives. They lived in the house three doors down from ours for almost twenty years, and Cissy asked me to find a buyer the day Ben died, which was also the day she moved back in with us. I found a buyer a little while later, a couple from Portland who came with their kids to teach at the elementary school. They moved away after the last one went off to college.* I think Pam regretted spilling so many beans about Cissy that night because she's turned down the few invitations we've made since. She's perfectly friendly when we run into her at the grocery store or gas station in Aberdeen, but she keeps her distance.

It's hard to believe it's been more than half a year since that morning Cissy pounded on the door of Room 6, sounding like some cop on TV. *Ma'am, I have a key so my knocking is just a formality. Ma'am, I'm reaching for my key and this door will open whether you want it to or not.* And just as she went for the key, the door opened and Jane stepped out. *Thank you,* she said, her hand waving a kind of apology as she pulled her tan coat on. She hurried away, down the steps toward the beach, where she stayed most of the rest of the day. Since then we've seen her wander down the beach for hours, barefoot, with her lace-up tennis shoes in one hand, the other arm usually wrapped around her waist. One morning at the end of the summer we thought she might have spent the night out there, because there was no light coming from her room, no clanking of water pipes or flushing toilet as there usually is. Her lights came on that evening and we saw the usual shadow passing across her curtains, so wherever she'd been the night before she made it back in one piece. I think she mainly lives on Cissy's cookies, because I've only twice seen her carrying bags from Laird's General Store into the room. Maybe she squirrels packets of nuts or candy bars in her jacket pockets when she goes down to the gas station ATM for cash each month, but if that's what she's doing, I've never seen any of it. What I have seen is Cissy lugging around a large thermos, the kind you carry soup or hot chocolate in. What's inside I don't know, but neither Kelly nor I ever saw that thermos before Jane came along. We've seen it out on the front stoop of Jane's room in the mornings, too. Cissy isn't one to gossip in general, but when we've tried to talk to her about Jane, she won't say more than that she keeps a tidy room. Even though it's well within our rights to want to know about the only long-term resident of the Moonstone—especially one who checked in under an alias and without ID—we always feel ashamed when we mention her in front of Cissy, and so we don't anymore. We just accept her as part of our lives, a quiet woman named Jane from somewhere east of here.

Lydia

The first call from Winton came in December. There are a few things to remember about that day, and she's tried, but the one thing she doesn't struggle to recollect was that the phone hadn't rung for weeks. It's an old, beige thing with thick buttons that make loud beeps when you press them, mounted on the wall by the door in the kitchen. It came with the rental she's living in, and carved into the doorframe next to it are phone numbers. She recognized a few when she moved in a little more than six years ago. Gary Beck's, for one; he had a funny relationship with her mother and would come by every once in a while with schnapps they'd drink in the kitchen. They both loved country music and listened to a station out of Hartford that played Loretta Lynn and Conway Twitty songs. When Lydia was a teenager, and even later, she thought their nights in the kitchen were the grimmest she could imagine. Smoking cigarettes, drinking peppermint schnapps, and turning up the radio when some sad song came on. Funny, she thinks now, remembering those nights, how things change when you look at them with older eyes.

She wonders if Gary Beck is even still alive. As far as she can remember, he never had a wife or kids or any relations. He wasn't involved in the volunteer fire department or church or any of the organizations that host spaghetti-and-meatball dinners at the elementary school to raise money. She never saw him outside of her mother's kitchen. He ran the post office in town until he had a stroke and was put in a state home for the elderly in Torrington. That all happened sixteen years ago, the year before her mother died. She'd told Lydia about Gary one morning on the phone but didn't convey any emotion, just enough interest to relay the facts. She doubts her mother ever went to visit him in Torrington. She never could quite figure out what their relationship was, but as attractive as her mother had been, and as much as she always dolled herself up each morning for work at the bank, she was pretty sure she'd shut the door on men after Lydia's father died. Still, she and her mother had never been what anyone would consider close, and so she wondered if anything more than companionship had gone on with Gary. He was harmless and he brought booze and always had a flattering thing to say when her mother opened the door to let him in. *Looking good tonight, Natalie* was as specific and flirtatious as he ever got. He was still coming around when Lydia and Luke moved in with her mother the year he was born, but after that she never saw him. It was hard for her to imagine who might have needed Gary Beck's number often enough to carve it into this wall. Maybe someone who worked at the post office. Maybe some other old gal he'd bring schnapps to and listen to country songs with. When she looked at the numbers gouged into the pine doorframe, she hoped so. She hoped he had a different one every night.

The other names could be anyone's—*Lisa, Matthew, Evelyn*. Only Gary Beck had the honor of his last name carved into the wood. And then there's the one number she can never forget. Her former mother-in-law's, Connie Morey. The Moreys must have had that same number since telephones were first installed in Litchfield County. The family had been in their old, broken-down house off Main Street since the late 1800s. They built it themselves, as they were all quick to tell you, and were still there. On the wall it just says *Connie* and those same digits Lydia used to dial when she was in high school, when Earl Morey was, for a short time, the only person she wanted to speak to or see. He was jumpy and mischievous, a soccer player with a big bush of red hair on his head. He loved the Grateful Dead and ice fishing and smoking pot and could mimic anyone he laid eyes and ears on for more than a minute. His favorite target was his older brother, Mike, who had a lisp and was not very bright. He also did a blistering impersonation of Lydia's mother, which it took her only one time to overhear from her bedroom to run him out of the apartment. Still, she loved him, but more than him she loved the idea of his family, which was not by any stretch of imagination wealthy—most of them electricians and housepainters and grounds-keepers at Harkness, the boarding school just over the town line in Bishop. It was and is their size and longevity that made them formidable. *There is safety in numbers,* Lydia's mother would say as she blew clouds of menthol smoke through the kitchen from behind the Formica table where she sat each night with her schnapps, like a general at her battle station making speeches to the troops. *I know because I've been out on my own for so long. Even before your father died a hundred years ago, it was just us. Just him and me against the world.*

Safety was not what attracted Lydia to Earl Morey. What she loved about him was that he made her laugh. Sometimes she'd laugh so hard she couldn't breathe, which would egg him on more. In high school, he had a short fuse, was a bit of a bully, and more than a few times was called off the soccer field for instigating fights with players on the other teams. That mean streak made Lydia nervous sometimes, but she told herself he was all talk, harmless, a showboat. And besides, no one could make her laugh as hard as he could. She experienced that laughter as a kind of exorcism. It quieted the voices of the girls at school who whispered behind her back and drowned out her mother's tipsy rants, and for a brief spell there was nothing but heaving lungs, pounding heart, and tears running down her cheeks.

She laughed with Earl for a while before they got married and not much after. After high school Earl went to work with his brothers on the maintenance crew at Harkness and joined the volunteer fire department. Within a few months, he stopped coming home for dinner. He'd go straight from work to the firehouse or to the Tap, where he'd eat beef jerky and potato chips. He'd come in after ten, drunk and cranky about something or someone. He'd pinch Lydia's ass and tell her to lay off the snacks. And soon he just called her Snacks. First at home and then in front of his family. His father thought it was funny. *Toughen up, girl,* he said to her at Christmas dinner that first year, *you know how he is*. And then there were the nights, in the beginning once every six weeks or two months, and then later every weekend, when he'd come home smashed and wake her up, speaking gibberish. Whether she responded or not, sat up in bed or curled into her pillow pretending to sleep, the result was the same. A hard blow either to the side of her head or her body. Usually, it was just one. Two at the most. And sometimes afterward he would grab her by the shoulders and shake her violently. Mostly it would be dark, so she wouldn't see him, but the few times he turned on a light or the moon outside would brighten the room enough, she would see a face so tortured and far away it was as if he were possessed, like some kind of zombie demon. She knew by then that the only thing capable of driving a demon away was another one; so when she recognized something that could drive Earl and most likely the rest of the town away, she didn't hesitate. That their demon would be her son was the awful consequence, but she didn't think she had a choice. Which was not how other people saw it, certainly not her mother or Connie Morey, who is long dead and whose number is still, like some threat from the underworld, carved into the wood next to Lydia's phone.

She's turned the ringer down as low as it goes, but she still jumps every time it rings. Ever since the morning when she got the phone call from Betty Chandler. *He's done it now, Lydia,* is what she said, clipped and cold and distant as if she were reporting that the high school football team was on a losing streak. *You need to get over to June Reid's house right away,* she added before hanging up. Betty Chandler and Lydia grew up together, went to the same kindergarten, elementary, and high school. They were even best friends one summer and fall when they were twelve—making barrettes with pink and blue ribbons and selling them for a dollar each—but when Betty's chubby older brother, Chip, tried to kiss Lydia, unsuccessfully, after the eighth-grade dance and then told people she let him go to third base, Betty turned on her and spread rumors that she was loose. Just like that, based on so very little, she became her enemy and managed to stay so for more than thirty years. Later, when Luke was born and Earl had thrown Lydia out, her mother said she'd heard Betty telling people she'd been accepting money to have sex with the migrant workers at Morgan Farm across the state line in Amenia, the ones who came from Mexico or the Caribbean every season to pick apples, and that's how she'd gotten pregnant. Her mother asked her if it was true. As painful as that was, Lydia never blamed her mother or any of them. She knew when she realized she was pregnant that if her baby's skin was even half as dark as its father's, she would be cast as the hussy. She never refuted any of the stories, never told anyone the truth, not even Luke, and when he was old enough he didn't want anything to do with her, let alone a father who had been kept a secret all his life. There were good reasons for keeping his father a secret. And if they weren't good, they were, she believed for a long time, necessary. Only one marriage would be upended by this baby and it would be hers.

Many times she came close to leaving, throwing

Luke in her car and driving away. But somehow she got used to the snickering whispers in the grocery store, the nasty gazes from the women, and the lewd once-overs from the men. One year became two, became five, became so many she couldn't count them. After Earl there were other men, but most didn't amount to much more than a few boozy sleepovers. Only Rex, who turned up many years later, stuck around long enough to look like a future, but the wreckage he left in his wake cured Lydia of ever again expecting one. After Rex, there was no more going to places like the Tap on weekends, no more men, and no more hope left that her life would ever happen any differently than it had.

Beyond visiting Luke in prison in the Adirondacks the one time and going to Atlantic City for her honeymoon with Earl, she'd never left Wells. *Some trees love an ax,* a drunk old-timer mumbled one night at the Tap, back when she still went there, and something in what he said rang true, but when she later remembered what he'd said, she disagreed and thought instead that the tree gets used to the ax, which has nothing to do with love. It settles into being chipped away at, bit by bit, blade by blade, until it doesn't feel anything anymore, and then, because nothing else can happen, what's left crumbles to dust.

After Luke died, the phone rang a lot. The funeral home, the insurance company, the bank, the police.

There were consoling calls, too, but mostly from people in Luke's life, not hers; people who adored him and worked with him, some who were in jail with him, a few old girlfriends, ones she'd never met, and a few guys who used to swim with him in high school, his old coaches. She heard their voices as if they came from the end of a long tunnel. Their words were like echoes, and often she would hold the phone away until she sensed the talking about to come to an end. She did her best to be polite, but it was hard to hear from strangers about her son's life, which she barely knew and had only just begun to be included in again.

Everyone she worked for called. The Moodys, the Hammonds, Peggy Riley, the Tucks, the Hills, and the Masseys, who owned the bed-and-breakfast in Salisbury where she used to drive each day to change beds, clean linens, and scrub the toilets and tubs. Even Tommy Ball called, though she hadn't seen him in years. All of them offered their condolences and told her to take her time and to please just let them know when she was ready to come back. She never called any of them. But she did take her time, *all of it,* she mumbled to herself more than a few times. From the age of thirteen until the morning Betty Chandler called her, Lydia had worked nearly every day of her life. From that moment forward, she was done. She figured that with the little money she had saved, there was enough to pay her living expenses for a year or so, and carry the minimum payments on her two credit cards if she had to use them to pay for food. Without having to go to work, she barely ever drove, so she didn't have to pay for gas. Propane and electric were included in her rent, which was only four hundred dollars a month, and the phone and cable bills were the cheapest possible.

It turned out later that Luke had a life insurance policy and Lydia was, inexplicably, the beneficiary. He also had a will, the kind you download from the Internet and get notarized, which he did. He left Lydia what he had—his savings, his land-scaping company, and his belongings, which, because he'd been living at June's, were destroyed. Between the insurance and the savings and the twenty thousand the Waller brothers paid her for the landscaping business—two trucks, a few wheelbarrows, a backhoe, and a pile of tools— she could exist as she lived now for a long time without working. For most of her life she had dreamed of the day she wouldn't have to stoop and scrub and haul and shine for other people. And so it came. One more demon replacing another.

June never called, not once. She hugged Lydia briefly at Luke's funeral but left town before she could say anything. Lydia wasn't surprised given how she behaved the morning Betty Chandler called. She'd done what Betty had instructed her to do and went straight to June's. She dropped the phone and in her slippers and robe drove the three miles to Indian Pond Road. June was squatting next to the mailbox, doubled over and away from the house, just at the top of the short, curving asphalt driveway. Lydia got out of her car and went toward her. Around them swarmed what looked like hundreds of firemen and police officers and EMTs. As she came closer, June turned her face away as if avoiding a hot flame and, as she did, held her arm up and flicked her hand toward Lydia, the way you wave away an unwanted animal, or a beggar. It was chilling, even in that unreal scene, to be greeted this way by a woman who had only ever shown her kindness. It is that gesture she remembers most clearly from that morning. Not Betty Chandler's heartless phone call, not the red flashing lights, not the army of stunned emergency workers, not the police officer telling her that her son was dead. It was June's hand, sending her away, the first signal that everything was about to change, had already changed, and that she was about to find out how. Those flicking, flapping fingers still jump before her eyes like a black flag snapping in the wind, commemorating all that was over. But Lydia never blamed her. Not only were her losses greater than Lydia's that day, if losses are measured in people, but June was the one who saw it happen. Whatever she had gone through, whatever she had seen, meant that Lydia was no longer bearable.

She assumed that June blamed Luke, like so many others had. But the truth was she had no idea. What Lydia knew was that in addition to the agony of losing Luke, there was a hard and recurring stab of pain from missing June—so strange to miss another woman—this woman who she never believed she could relate to or like, let alone love. And Lydia still loved her. She had given her back her son. When June met Luke, Lydia had not spoken to her son in over eight years. Not a word since that afternoon in the freezer section of the grocery store. One year and then eight. And then June.

She appeared on Lydia's doorstep. After no one answered her knocking, she waited on the front porch. When Lydia came home that afternoon, she saw a woman, roughly her own age, or older, who looked like every woman she'd ever worked for. Faded jeans, fit, simple but tailored cotton T-shirt, blond hair with streaks of silver pulled back in a ponytail, flashes of expensive metal at her wrists and throat and ears. She thought at first she was some weekender from the city looking to hire a housecleaner. When she introduced herself as the woman in Luke's life—*We've been living together this year,* she said—Lydia immediately asked her to leave. She knew about June Reid. She knew where she lived and where she was from. She'd even once driven by her old stone house on Indian Pond Road between the apple orchards and the fields that led to the Unification Church property. It was surrounded by old pine and locust trees, and in the winter it looked like a Christmas card. She'd overheard people she worked for, people who knew June Reid from the city, mention how she'd taken up with a local guy, much younger. And then Bess Tuck, one of her employers who lived in the city during the week, asked her point-blank whether Lydia knew whom her son was dating. When Lydia answered that she did not, Bess told her the woman was someone who'd had dinner *in this very house,* she emphasized, as if it were the most spectacular and impossible coincidence.

Lydia knew about June Reid but had never seen her. And here she was. As much as she'd wondered how Luke was and what he was doing and whom with, she knew right away she couldn't bear this woman telling her about her son. It was as if she had taken her place or succeeded where she had failed. But even if the kind of love they had was a totally different kind of love than a mother and son's, she didn't want it rubbed in her face by someone whose motives for being with a man so young could not be good. *Leave,* she said to her as she struggled to unlock the door to her apartment. *I don't know who you are and I don't want to. Go away.*

June came back a few weeks later and again Lydia rushed inside. But the next time she came, Lydia didn't duck into her apartment or tell her to go. She stood on the porch and let her speak. It embarrasses her to remember, but she was flattered this elegant woman was so determined to spend time with her. After a little while, she asked her in. She stayed and she talked, and she came again, and after that again. Eventually, Luke came with her. The first few times he barely spoke, and Lydia, terrified she'd say the wrong thing and cause him to storm out, kept quiet. Lydia remembers June teasing Luke about the kids he hired—*Perverts, pickpockets, and potheads,* she'd chant—and each time would get a reaction. He'd try to get mad, but when he did, she would poke him in the stomach or under his arms and he would, against his will, melt. During those first few sessions, June's light joking was the only sound to break the silence, and as difficult as it was to see Luke so at ease with a woman her own age, she was grateful. Slowly, after a few visits, he began to talk about work, even ask Lydia questions about the people she cleaned for. And then one morning, before Lydia left for the day, he showed up alone. They sat on the bottom step of her porch, mostly in silence, and watched two teenage boys scrape paint from the fence of a house on Lower Main Street. Eventually Lydia turned toward Luke and cautiously placed her hand on his shoulder. She began to speak, *Luke, I . . .* but he interrupted her, rushing his words, which sounded as if he'd rehearsed them. *We'll be okay. . . . I don't ever want to talk about it because there's nothing you can say to change what happened. And I don't want you to try. I'll never understand. I don't want to. But we'll be okay.* Before she could respond, he hugged her— quickly, the first time in years, his neck against her face, his smell, his skin, all of a sudden so close. He stood, and as he turned toward his truck to leave, he stumbled awkwardly and nearly fell. *I have to,* he started to say, righting himself, then pausing a beat, *stop drinking in the morning,* a smile flaring, his eyes bright. This was less than one year before he died. Nothing, and then so much, then nothing.

After those first few weeks following the accident, Lydia stopped picking up the phone. Sometimes she'd leave the apartment, walk down to the town green and back to avoid it. Other times she'd just let it ring and ring. She'd turn the volume up on the television to drown the sound out, or if someone kept calling, she'd get in the shower and turn on the radio that hung from the showerhead. Eventually, the phone went quiet.

When the first call came from Winton, she picked up. It was the day she ran from the women at the coffee shop. When she came home that night, she sat down at the kitchen table. That

87

first flash of anger when she'd heard the women gossiping frightened her, and panic drove her home. But the longer she sat in the kitchen and the more she replayed what she'd heard, the more that anger returned, and she felt again the hot violence from before. Something about those women—no more careless or cruel than anyone else she'd ever come across, and probably less so than many—something about what they said and how they said it that made her want to hurt someone. That anger and the ugly fantasies it fueled had her shaking in the dark kitchen. She sat there for so long and so still that when the phone rang, she jumped to her feet. Even at its lowest volume it startled her, and she rushed across the kitchen to pick up. The voice on the other end was a man's, a younger man's. She was relieved it was no one she knew. He sounded British but with a lilt or swerve in the accent that she couldn't place. He asked if she was Lydia Morey, and when she said yes, he said, *Miss Lydia Morey, you've won the lottery.* Silly, she knew. Obviously some kind of scam, but she was caught off guard. *I don't win anything,* she said without thinking, then told him he must have the wrong person because she hadn't entered any lottery. As if anticipating her response, he said, *Sometimes we enter lotteries and do not know; for example, if you have a magazine subscription or a Triple A membership, you may have automatically been submitted for a lottery.* She told him she didn't have any magazine subscriptions and was not a member of anything, and then he laughed. A big, wide warm laugh. After that, he said her name, slowly. *Miss. Lydia. Morey.* He just said her name, the same one when spoken out loud at the coffee shop earlier had caused her to flee. As he said it, heat rippled across her chest. A funny bone she didn't even know was still there had been tickled, and something like a smile wrinkled her lips. Before she let him speak another word, she slammed the phone in its cradle.

June

There is no lake. She has been inching along this rock-strewn dirt road for hours, and there has been no sign of water, no cars, no humans, no evidence that she took the right exit after Missoula, or pointed the car in the right direction each time the almost-road forked. She is lost and alone and it does not matter. Nothing does, she thinks, not for the first time. She circles the idea again and again—that no choice she might make would have any impact on her or anyone else. Before now she would have felt exhilarated by the idea of existing without obligation or consequence, but the experience is nothing like she once imagined. This is a half-life, a split purgatory where her body and mind coexist but occupy separate realities. Her eyes look at what is ahead—the road, a fallen tree—but her mind scours the past, judges each choice made, relives every failure, roots out what she overlooked, took for granted, and didn't pay attention to. The present scarcely registers. The people she sees are not the ones pumping gas into the Subaru, passing her on the highway, or making change when they sell her bottles of water and peanuts at mini-marts and gas stations. Instead it is Luke, pleading with her in a kitchen that no longer exists; Lolly, shouting at the top of her fourteen-year-old lungs from across a restaurant table in Tribeca; Adam, looking up at her, shocked, a young girl's hand in his; Lydia stepping toward her that morning, before she knew what had happened, and the confusion and hurt on her face as June waved her off. She returns to these memories and replays them over and over, scrutinizes every remembered word, witnesses again each mistake. When she exhausts one, another appears. Another always does.

Her mind leaps to her childhood friend Annette. Annette lived two streets away in the same neighborhood in Lake Forest, and they spent their Saturday nights at each other's house, playing with Annette's collection of porcelain horses, listening to Shaun Cassidy and Jackson 5 records, making lists of where they would live when they grew up, what car they would drive, and what their husbands would look like. She remembers convincing Annette to come with her to sleepaway camp in New Hampshire the summer between fifth and sixth grades. Annette was timid, a careful creature who was reluctant to agree. For both it would be their first time away from home with-out parents, and Annette cited plenty of reasons not to go—the high school boys who lifeguarded at the club pool, an Arabian-horse show coming to Chicago. But June kept at her over the Christmas holiday, even convinced her mother to call and explain to Annette's protective mother the place where she herself had gone as a girl. June can't recall why it was so important she come with her, but remembers clearly the triptych of cousins from Beverly Hills who naturally and without ceremony established themselves at the top of the social pecking order from the first day. They had glamorous names—Kyle, Blaire, and Marin—and all three had the same feathered, shoulder-length, light brown hair.

On the second full day at camp, the Beverlys, as they had come to be known, asked June to switch her bunk with a chunky, gravel-voiced girl named Beth from Philadelphia. Beth and the Beverlys had been assigned the same cabin four down from June and Annette's, and Beth, the cousins explained, not only smelled like garlic but stared at them when they were changing. June's face prickles with heat as she remembers sneaking her sleeping bag and duffel to her new cabin while Annette ate lunch with the others in the lodge. Later that night, one of the counselors showed up at June's cabin with Annette and insisted on speaking to June. She hadn't believed Beth when she explained that June had asked her to switch bunks. June remembers Annette's face relaxing as she entered the cabin. She imagines what must have raced through her head in that moment— here was June, her best friend, the girl she traveled halfway across the country with, who knew everything there was to know about her and who was wearing the rope bracelet Annette made for her birthday two years ago. Here was June and she would clear everything up. June remembers how she attempted to be casual, to pretend that nothing important had transpired or changed. But as she stumbled through a rehearsed explanation that it seemed like a good idea to give each other space and meet new people, Annette's face froze. She looked at June as if she were regarding a complete stranger. It was not anger or hurt that registered on her pale, blank face. It was horror. June had, in that instant, transformed into someone she didn't know. June can see Annette shaking her head as if she had been hit from behind by a thrown rock. She can see her turn toward the cabin door and walk away as the Beverlys snickered from their bunks. Annette went home the next morning. They were twelve years old and the two girls never spoke again. That fall, when they returned to Lake Forest Country Day for the first day of sixth grade, Annette would not look at her.

June wonders what became of Annette's vast collection of porcelain horses. She took fastidious care of each one, dusting and polishing their glazed coats, gently brushing their manes and tails. There were dozens, maybe hundreds. Annette was an only child and had a playroom lined with white bookshelves loaded with those horses. She and her mother made special trips to antiques dealers in Springfield and Bloomington and Chicago to expand her collection. She had a real horse, too, a dark brown, gelding quarter horse she named Tilly, who was kept at a stable in Winnetka, but June was never invited there after school or on weekend mornings when Annette rode. June cannot remember the father clearly, only that he smoked a pipe, always wore a tie, and was rarely there.

After eighth grade, Annette and Tilly went East to a horsey boarding school in Virginia and June lost track of her. More than two decades later, after her divorce from Adam and after she'd moved to London, June was having lunch with a client, the American wife of a British banker, and when June's childhood in Lake Forest came up, the woman asked her if she remembered a girl named Annette Porter. She'd been a sorority sister of hers at Butler University in Indiana. *Great girl,* the woman said, and though it stung to hear Annette's name even all those years later, it was a relief to know she had been welcomed into a sisterhood somewhere and in that circle was considered great.

It never occurred to June before now what might have happened to Annette's mother when her daughter left home. She imagines the poor woman taking up Annette's duties dusting, polishing, and brushing the manes of each figurine. June pictures her now, all these years later, muttering to them, bringing them up to speed on the little neighborhood traitor who used to visit, the one who lured Annette to sleepaway camp and how she finally got what was coming to her.

Streaks of blue flash between the pines, and for a moment June struggles to remember where she is. She traces an imaginary map as she slows the car to a stop. Montana. Glacier National Park. Bowman Lake. She turns the engine off and watches the lake appear between the spaces in the trees. It reminds her of when Lolly would see a jumping light through the windows of the house in Connecticut at night and be convinced it was a UFO. She wouldn't rest until they'd gone outside to see, and of course it was always just a star above the trees, beyond the house, blinking in and out of view. Still, she would insist that she'd seen something extraordinary.

June gets out of the car and looks for a path. The pine forest is dense, and though it is early afternoon and midsummer, the air is chilly under the branches. She fetches her coat from the car and wraps it around her shoulders before stepping off the road. Pine needles crunch softly beneath her tennis shoes and birds holler as she makes her way toward a clearing that overlooks a narrow strip of rocky beach. From there she can see the entire lake, which is much longer than it is wide and swerves gently to the left as it stretches toward its end. Impossibly straight pines cover the low hills that swell from the waterline, and beyond them rise hulking stone mountains. The landscape reminds her of northern Scotland, though these hills are younger, she decides, less worn-out.

The sun dazzles the wind-chopped surface of the water and the effect is blinding. There is, briefly, nothing but light. She squints from reflex, but the rest of her surrenders, waits to be erased. It is a quick oblivion, snuffed out as swiftly as it arrives. A cloud barges across the sky and returns color and shape to the trees, the hills, the pebbled shore. She waits for the sun to flare again, and soon it does. She feels its heat—enormous, perfect—and shivers as it recedes. She stands and waits for the radiant nothing to return and, as she does, remembers a motel shower four or five days ago in Gary, Indiana, with water pressure so forceful she saw stars as she let it pummel the back of her neck and head. She stood there until the water went cold. She thinks of the morning in her car days ago, just over the North Dakota state line, when she woke to the sound of idling school buses and shouting. Stiff from sleeping in the front seat and only half-awake, she blinked toward children in T-shirts and shorts dragging backpacks and lunch boxes. She had no idea where or who she was or what she was seeing.

She looked at the light brick building, the buses, the American flag dangling from a white pole. Nothing was familiar. She was empty of memory, and instead of being frightened or upset, she was, dimly, without yet understanding why, relieved. The spell broke when she noticed her linen jacket bunched between the driver's seat and the car door. It took nothing more than the sight of the wrinkled fabric for every last memory to return, including pulling off the interstate late the night before, looking for a motel and instead finding a quiet spot in the parking lot next to the school.

More clouds gather and the surface of the water darkens. She can now see more clearly the long, rectangular shape of the lake. It is just as Lolly described to her in a postcard once. *Flawless*. That was the word she used. She had found a flawless place, the first on her journey across country after her freshman year in college, perhaps the first ever. She'd been gone for more than a month when the postcard arrived, the first and the last she would send June from the trip. It was one of just four missives Lolly had ever mailed to her and the only one June saved. The postcard had been in the house, tucked away in one of her address books, but June remembers clearly the image of the lake, the Kalispell, Montana, postmark, the stiff closing, the clipped, telegram-like sentences wedged between the postcard's edge and her London mailing address.

M., A flawless place. The first so far. Back in NY early August. Until soon, L.

The photo on the postcard had shown snow on the surrounding mountaintops, but now, under the summer sun, they are bare rock. This difference aside, the lake looks the same. Nothing changes here, June thinks, but then remembers an article she'd skimmed years ago about global warming and the gradual disappearance of the glaciers from Glacier National Park. Looking at this lake and these mountains, she wonders when the glacier that made this place was last in residence, how long it lasted. Did some trace of it still remain when Lolly was here?

Lolly was eighteen years old when she looked at this lake. Eighteen and angry and newly free. She had lived with her father in New York the last three years of high school. Her choice to stay with him after the divorce was never questioned or challenged, though it took the wind out of June when Adam, not Lolly, told her. It never occurred to her that Lolly would stay in New York. But when June spoke to her the next day, Lolly made it clear that just as June had made her decision to leave them for London, she had in turn made hers. They spent Christmas together at the house in Connecticut the first year after the divorce, but it ended abruptly with Adam driving back to the city on Christmas Day after Lolly opened her presents. There had been no fight, no dramatic blowup, just Adam's restlessness and Lolly's hostile quiet. She begged her father to take her back to the city, but he insisted she stay since June would be in the States for only two weeks and they should spend time together. Lolly retreated to her room upstairs and she and June spent the remaining days silent and on separate floors. Lolly refused to eat with June and would instead take bowls of granola and cup after cup of coffee upstairs. June stayed in London the following Christmas, and in the years when Lolly was at Vassar, June and Adam worked out alternating Christmas Eve and Christmas Day custody.

Lolly never came to London. In five years she never saw the gallery June opened. Never saw the small carriage house in Islington where she lived. Never accepted any of June's invitations to join her in London and travel on to Europe or Scotland or Ireland. She returned one out of every seven or eight phone calls, just enough to keep from creating a crisis and instigating a serious discussion. She hardly ever wrote e-mails before texting came along, and even then the missives either explained her silence or signaled more. *Will call this weekend. Buried. Can't make it to NY next week when you're there. Sorry.* There were a lot of sorrys.

The sun returns, the lake shines again. The birds have stopped yelling and June hears Lolly's voice rise above the noises of a restaurant the night she and Adam explained what was going to happen. June had just finished calmly describing how she and Adam were getting divorced, would remain friends, and that she would be opening a gallery in London for her boss. Lolly, June explained, could come with her or stay in New York to finish high school. *Liar!* Lolly shouted from across the table of the restaurant on Church Street where they ate most Sunday nights after returning from Connecticut. The whole place went silent. *You lied to us! You did, you lied! You promised to be a mother and wife and now you are choosing to be neither.* Lolly glared in silence before running to the bathroom. June can see her, the table between them, Adam at her side, mute, Lolly's eyes tear-less, desperately scanning her mother's face for something familiar, anything she could recog-nize. June knows these eyes. They are Annette's, Luke's, Lydia's. People who when they last looked at her saw a stranger.

June never argued custody with Adam. She never told Lolly how Adam had been accused of sexual harassment at NYU, how they had to settle and by doing so wiped out their savings and nearly half of the inheritance her father had left her when she was in her twenties. The only thing June hung on to was the house in Connecticut, which she and Adam had paid off only the year before. It was the unexpected financial setback, June told herself then, that kept her pushing for bigger and bigger sales at the gallery, landing more lucrative artists and needing to fly around the globe for both. But she knows now she couldn't face what was happening at home, what was going on with Adam. She knew a fire was behind the smoke of accusation even though she wanted to believe him when he insisted the student who'd filed suit was unstable. Lolly had been a kid at the time and June chose to believe Adam. For that belief to sustain, Lolly could never find out, which she never did. Or if she had, she never let on. June wonders if all the secret-keeping back then explained why, years later, she covered up for Adam again. Had it become second nature? Lolly also never knew about the call June received from her friend Peg, who was, she whispered, at that moment watching Adam hold hands with a young girl at a restaurant in Long Island City. *Stay out of sight,* June told Peg before scribbling down the address and beelining out of the gallery and onto Fifty-seventh Street to hail a cab.

The restaurant was on the roof of an old loft building on Jackson Avenue, near PS1. As June entered the freight elevator, she tried to imagine how Adam had found his way here. How he must have thought it was another planet, this stomping ground for young hipsters and musicians. A frontier for the creative and the broke, but most important, a place where no one knew him and where he'd never get caught. June spotted Adam right away and was relieved that Peg hadn't made a mistake. The relief was, at last, the absence of the doubt she'd had for years, even before the lawsuit. The relief was that he would now get caught in a manner that left no room for explanation or double-talk. Before approaching the table, June saw the months ahead. A divorce with terms she would dictate, accepting the long-on-the-table offer from her boss, Patrick, to open a gallery in London that she hadn't until now allowed herself to take seriously. She watched Adam stare at the girl while she tapped on her PalmPilot with her free hand, and for the first time June could see him in his natural state. Not the one he fashioned to keep family harmony. He looked old, surrounded here by flannels and tattoos and full beards, hunched over this distracted girl who was only a few years older than their daughter. This was her husband. The man she'd once loved and wished to build a life with. The man she still loved, despite years of resenting him. This, she recognized, was her freedom. She could see it all as she stepped toward the small table along the wall. The girl with the wide face and black hair, Adam's fingers on the inside of her wrist, the table covered in corn bread.

She could see the future that day, but she failed to see Lolly. Failed to think through the next steps carefully. Failed to resist Adam's desperate plea not to tell their daughter about the affair and failed to see how not telling her the truth would shape everything between them after. She moved too fast toward that table and she moved too fast after—to court, to agree with Adam, to London. She knows that if she could retrace her steps after that phone call from Peg, rethink every decision that followed, she would not be standing on the shore of a lake in the middle of nowhere. And everyone would be alive.

June takes a few steps back from the lake and leans against the closest pine. Near its trunk patches of thick green moss cover the ground like tossed pillows. She tries to imagine Lolly in this place five years ago. Did she stand right here? Did she stop at the first sight of water, too, and find her way to this clearing? Did she rest on this moss? Did she look to the lake and see her mother as she now sees Lolly? Is this where she began to forgive her? And if she were alive, could she possibly forgive her now?

June sits down on the damp moss and draws her knees to her chest. There is no peace for her here. She remembers the morning in North Dakota two days before when she decided to find this place. Bowman Lake. These two words came to her as she watched what must have been summer-school students filing noisily across the parking lot into the school. *Bowman Lake,*

Glacier National Park, Montana. She saw again the small, black capital letters at the bottom of the postcard spelling the location, and as the school buses shut their doors and lumbered toward the road, she could see the pristine lake, its glassy surface reflecting a cloudless sky. She remembered Lolly's careful handwriting on the other side, and as she read the short sentences over and over, she understood where she needed to be. A place where her daughter had found no flaw.

Rebecca

Her car just sits there. A newish Subaru wagon with Connecticut plates. Black, like all the cars I remember there. I guess we could call in the license-plate number if we really wanted to know who she is, but it feels too sneaky, and on some level I think each of us—me, Kelly, Cissy—feels as if she has, even though she barely speaks, appointed us her protectors. From what or from whom I don't know, but from something. So tracing her plates—however one does that, I have no idea—or sleuthing around in any way feels like breaking the deal we struck when we agreed to let her stay here anonymously. If we'd had a problem then, we could have refused her, but we chose not to and so she stays here, whoever she is.

At Christmas, one of Kelly's brothers came down from Seattle with his wife and sons, and we opened presents Christmas morning and cooked a big dinner that afternoon. Kelly left a note under the door to Room 6 inviting her to join our four o'clock supper, but she never responded or came, not that we expected her to. Cissy left a tin of her sugar cookies topped with chocolate and caramel in addition to what looked like a loaf of the same banana-and-blueberry bread she made for us. *At least she's getting some fruit,* Kelly joked, but for the first time looking genuinely worried.

I've been worried since the day she arrived. Something about the way she dragged herself when she walked, her exhaustion, and the limit to how much she could engage, the way her eyes were open physically but in every other way were shut. It was a look I recognized. *What if she's come to die here? What then?* I asked Kelly after the New Year. *Then she's come here to die and there's nothing we can or should do about it,* she answered, matter-of-fact, as usual. *But if she dies and it comes out that we checked her in without ID or a credit card, won't we get in trouble? Isn't there some law?* Kelly looked at me in that way that she does, that way that makes me feel like a ridiculous child who's asked to stay up an hour past her bedtime. She looked at me this same way when I first brought up leaving Seattle and moving here. And she kept on looking at me this way until she finally came around. One thing about Kelly is that although she's deeply set in her ways—up at six fifteen every morning, black coffee and a boiled egg with the newspaper down the hatch by seven, Levi's cords and L.L. Bean flannel shirts and nothing but nothing else —she is also brave. If she has a good enough reason to set a new course, she will. In this case the good enough reason was me.

I wanted to leave Seattle because of my friend Penny. She was my closest friend and I'd known her since I was a little kid. We grew up a few doors down from each other in Worcester, Massachusetts, in big Catholic families, and went to the University of Massachusetts together after high school. We never had a fling because neither of us could back then admit to ourselves or each other that we were gay. Not in high school, not in college, and not for a while after. You have to remember, this was the seventies and early eighties, and though it's not that long ago, for gays it's like another millennium. Especially in Worcester, Massachusetts, and especially in our neighborhood, which was 100 percent Catholic and 100 percent straight, at least on the surface. After Penny and I graduated from college, we went to New York. She wanted to work in advertising, and neither of us could face returning to Worcester. I had always planned on Boston, but Penny could be pushy when she wanted to be, and so New York it was. We lived on the Upper East Side at first, and in many ways, not good ones, it felt like places we'd been. Mostly families, straight couples, and hard-partying college graduates living five to an apartment. It took us a while but we found our way to other parts of the city, and eventually to other women like us. But, boy, we were slow! Or at least I was. Once she found it, Penny took to that scene quick and within a few months had a girlfriend, a job as a bartender at Henrietta Hudson, and was on a softball team. I didn't like the bars so much, the hard drinking and the drugs. Those girls were wild. Most of them, like us, were from somewhere else and had whole lifetimes of loneliness and anger stored up. Once they hit the city, and each other, they let it all out, and often it was messy. Penny started to get messy, and after she moved in with her girlfriend, a young girl named Chloe, we drifted apart. I was working at the Lowell Hotel on East Sixty-third at the time as a check-in clerk. It's a beautiful art deco gem, and many of the rooms are actually apartments where people live either year-round or when they are in town for shopping or shows or business. I loved the order of the place, the fresh flowers, the crisp staff uniforms, the history. It felt like nothing bad could ever happen there. I got promoted twice in that first year, and by the time I was twenty-six I was an assistant manager. Nothing had ever really worked so well for me—not childhood, school, family, or the gay scene in New York. In all these places I had always been the odd duck. But at the Lowell, I fit. I knew where I was useful and where I wasn't, and so I spent most of my time there, on and off the clock. Meanwhile, Penny was bartending and boozing and giving up on her dream of working in adver-tising. She'd gone on some interviews and sent her résumé around when we first got to

New York, but once she moved in with Chloe, all that stopped. Chloe had been raised in Brooklyn by two hippie parents and was out and proud since high school. She was nineteen and had already dropped out of Barnard College by the time she met Penny.

It wasn't until Penny's first overdose on heroin that I began to understand what was going on. Even though it had been over a month since we'd seen each other, I was still her emergency contact at the bar, so two days after she hadn't showed up I got a call. I tracked down Chloe, who tried at first to cover it up. She floundered with a story that Penny was home with the flu, but only after I showed up at their apartment on the Lower East Side and pounded on the door did she finally tell me the truth. Penny was on the psych ward at Bellevue, where she had been transferred after detoxing in the emergency room. The hospital wouldn't release her for at least a few more days. Chloe told me later that night that she wanted Penny to move out, that she was a disaster, and that the whole scene was too much for her to handle. Never mind that it was Chloe who'd introduced Penny to heroin, we packed Penny's things and moved them into my studio in Murray Hill. Chloe gave me a letter to give to Penny, breaking things off, I assume, since I never read it. Whatever she wrote convinced Penny not to try to change Chloe's mind.

Penny lived with me the rest of that year. There'd be two more overdoses, hundreds of dollars stolen from my wallet, and a suicide attempt before Penny finally agreed to go to a rehab I found outside Seattle. I flew with her there and stayed the first few days, but then returned to New York to my job. She stayed in that rehab for eight months and then moved for a year and a half into a nearby sober house with other women in recovery. By then I'd been out to Seattle to visit her a dozen times. Penny's family, like mine with me, wanted nothing to do with her when she came out to them, which was the Christmas after our first year in New York. It's not an original story except that we decided to tell our parents the same night. We timed it to dinner, which was six o'clock in both of our houses. In my case, my father left the table and my mother wept into her napkin. In her case, they asked her to leave the house and come back only when she had, her father said, *cleaned up her act.* She knocked on my door that night, slept in a sleeping bag on my bedroom floor, and we went back to New York together first thing in the morning. My mother eventually came around, but only after my father had died, and even then she asked that I not rub it in her face by telling her about girlfriends. Meeting them, and of course there only ever was one, was out of the question. So she died doing the best she could, but in the end we barely knew each other.

After that Christmas, Penny and I were, for each other, clearly the only people we could count on. Besides my job at the Lowell and the people I worked with there, Penny was my entire world. Every free weekend or vacation I had I was on a plane to Seattle to see her. On one of those trips I met Kelly. She was the manager at the Holiday Inn not far from Penny's sober house, and one night after I'd flown all day from New York, she checked me in. She was agitated, I could tell, but professional. I found out later she was working the check-in desk because one of her employees had called in sick at the last minute, and as a result she had to miss her nephew's basketball game. There she was, in her gray cords and green Holiday Inn blazer, wrinkling her nose like she always does when she's pissy. I remember watching her for a long time, her head down, red hair jammed into a ponytail with loose strands floating from her head like spun gold, processing my credit card and mumbling under her breath all the while. Finally, she looked up, and for the first time I saw her eyes—green and gold and flashing like Christmas trees from her freckle-splattered face. I don't know how someone like me, who had never before even had a girlfriend, could recognize love when it arrived, but I did. I'd dated a little in New York, but women scared me. They were either too brash and manly or drank too much. People weren't as open then either, so if I was attracted to someone, most of the time I didn't know if she was gay. And I've never been the aggressive one, never the one to make a move or give someone my number. So I worked all hours and in my free time talked to Penny on the phone and listened to her tell me about the meetings she went to and the sober women she lived with. And I went to see her. This went on for a couple years before that night at the Holiday Inn. I saw those Christmas-tree eyes and my life changed.

Three nights? she asked as she looked at my reservation. I don't think I managed more than a nod in response. *You happen to be free for a drink or a bite any one of those nights?* Just like that. After two words and a nod she asked me out. Kelly has never been shy, and thank God. I nodded again, and the next night she took me to a steak house near the harbor, and the night after that she made me cream of asparagus soup and a big salad with pears and walnuts and chunks of avocado. It was the best salad I'd ever had. I know it sounds insane, but the next night I was on a plane to New York drafting my resignation. I was twenty-eight and had been alone for a long time. I watched people my age at the Lowell pair off and make plans, throw dinner parties and go on vacations together, get engaged. I knew I didn't want to be alone anymore. I moved in with Kelly two months later and took a job at the Westin Hotel as the night manager. It was a far fall down the scale from the Lowell, but I didn't care. I was with Kelly and near Penny, who was clean, living in a sober house, and working in ad sales at a local newspaper. For a long while I was what most people would describe as happy. I didn't feel that low, lonely ache I'd felt in my gut my whole life—growing up in Worcester, at school in Amherst, and in New York, especially on the weekends after Penny left. For the first time in my life, I was happy. We didn't have a ton of friends—Kelly had her brothers and nephews, and I had Penny. Outside that circle we liked plenty of people well enough, colleagues and neighbors and acquaintances, but we mainly kept our own company. We never got wrapped up in the gay scene, which was for young people, and we weren't young anymore. We had our small tribe and that was enough.

Kelly and Penny bickered sometimes, like sisters, and every so often a dinner would end abruptly, Penny getting worked up over something Kelly had said, usually political, and storming out. But Kelly adored Penny and was always the first to show up to her house if a pipe burst or if she needed help painting a room. She was always at our house with this girlfriend or that—none of them stuck—watching movies, cooking meals, bragging about her softball-team victories, complaining about work. She didn't have far to go since she lived two doors down to the right from the end of our street. Kelly always used to say that if the wind was just right, she could throw a Frisbee from our stoop and hit Penny's house.

And then, out of the blue, a couple of kids climbed through Penny's window and raped and strangled her to death. She was alone, the girl she was seeing—she always liked them young—was still in college and asleep at her dorm that night. It was late, three or four o'clock in the morning, and no one heard her screaming. I still have nightmares about what she must have gone through, how terrified she had to have been. For a long time I didn't speak beyond muttering. Neither did Kelly. We just sort of coexisted in near silence for months. We went to our jobs, came home, went to bed after eating something. The world had changed and we with it. Penny's family did not come to her funeral. A friend from New York came, and a girl we knew in college, too, the staff at the paper where Penny had become associate publisher, her softball team, her sober friends. And us. I was a mess, so Kelly spoke and Penny's boss did, too. And then it was over. There are no words precise enough to describe how wide and empty the world is when you lose someone that matters to you as much as Penny did to me. Every effort suddenly seems useless. I made it through the funeral and a few months after. But the mornings got tougher as time went by, and it became more and more difficult to get out of bed. I started calling in sick to work and eventually just said I was taking a vacation. One week turned into three, and the manager of the hotel called and said we needed to have a talk. Over the phone, without even so much as meeting with him, I told him I quit. Said those two short words, hung up the phone, and rolled back into my pillow. He called Kelly at work and told her what had happened before I could. He told her that he understood I was going through a tough time and that the hotel was happy to give me a leave and help out in any way they could, but he wasn't accepting my resignation. Kelly came straight home, threw a handful of sweaters and socks and toiletries into a bag, picked me up out of the bed—in my sweat-pants and T-shirt—and carried me out the front door and into the passenger seat of her CRX. *Change of scene* is all she said as she started driving— as much to herself, I think, as to me. She pulled onto 101 and headed south, along the coast. By the time we got to Astoria, just over the Oregon border, the sun was setting over the Pacific. We stayed the night at a little bed-and-breakfast, but the town was spooky—steep hills stacked impossibly with ramshackle houses, all of it tilting above a ghosty wharf. We left that morning and drove back up 101 to the edge of Grays Harbor. North of Aberdeen along 109, it's all beach. Little houses, a few motels and beach. And above it all the widest sky I'd ever seen. It was May and still chilly, but we pulled over to the side of the road and walked past the dunes to the water. Kelly told me to take my shoes off even though the sand was freezing cold. The wind was wild, and as we walked, we leaned into it to keep moving forward. It was the first real effort I'd made in months, leaning in, not allowing myself to be blown back or down. The hard, cold sand beneath my feet felt good, and I remembered I had a body and that it could feel. We walked along the surf's edge for twenty minutes or so and eventually we saw the Moonstone. From the beach it looked abandoned, but as we got closer, we saw a few lights on in the office and a housekeeper dragging a vacuum between rooms. The place was flaking with old paint and for the most part empty, but I was struck by the way it squatted at the edge of the beach, under that enormous blue sky and before the vast Pacific. It sat there, ugly and unbudging, the sandy wind whipping along its rusted gutters. I thought of Penny.

We stayed that night in Room 6, where Jane is now, but long before the good mattress. And then, after a few weeks of convincing Kelly, we sold our house, quit our jobs, and cashed in our 401(k)'s early. During that time we came back to

Moclips twice and haggled with the Hillworths, who'd been trying to unload the place for years but had a hard time letting go. Eventually, we bought the Moonstone and the Hillworths' house next door and all the scratched and broken-down furniture in both. Kelly and I had worked in hotels our entire adult lives, and now we owned one that needed us as much as we needed it. Kelly's brothers thought we were crazy, but they knew once we'd made up our minds there was no turning back.

That was over four years ago and I still think about Penny every day. I talk to her when I walk the beach and I ask her what she would do about this or that. I've asked her about Jane and if I should worry, and in the roar of the ocean I hear her say keep watch but let her be. Each time I head back up the beach and come upon the Moonstone, I remember the first time I saw it and Kelly's face smiling at me in the crazy wind. And later that night, the two of us crawling into bed in that room that sits so close to the sea. After we turned out the lights, I tucked under the blankets and thanked God. For Kelly, for this life. And for Penny, who helped me survive growing up in Worcester, getting through college, and convincing me to move to New York. And into the dark I thanked Penny directly, for being my best friend, for agreeing to go to rehab in Seattle, for getting sober, and for staying out there long enough for me to check in that night at the Holiday Inn. I shivered as I imagined all the possible outcomes if any one thing had happened differently along the way. If my parents had moved us to some other neighborhood in Worcester when I was a kid. If Penny had never met Chloe and never tried heroin. If I'd picked the Econo Lodge or the Days Inn that night in Seattle. If I'd left New York one day before, or after. If Kelly's employee hadn't called in sick. If Penny's girlfriend had slept at her house instead of the dorms the night those kids turned up. If Penny had locked her windows. I curled into Kelly and burrowed as deeply as I could into her back. I remember the tissue-thin, pale yellow T-shirt she wore, pressing my face to it and feeling her warm skin on the other side. And I remember thinking this is what it feels like to be home. Here. In the space around and between us. This fabric, this skin, this smell, this woman.

For most of that night I was awake, wondering at it all, the pattern that seemed to emerge when I laid out every fluke and chance encounter, puzzling through all the possible signs and meanings; but any trace of a design disintegrated when I remembered the chaos and brutality of the world, the genocide and the natural disasters, all the agony. I never felt so small, so humbled, by the vastness of the universe and the fragility of life. I studied the water-stained ceiling in the room and imagined the things it had seen, the people. Who else had huddled here, pressed into someone they loved as if they were the last thing on earth that mattered? Who else prayed that morning would never come? Prayed they'd never have to leave this bed and let go.

That night, the moon glowed through the curtains of the locked window, its storybook light dancing a path to the horizon, to the other side of the world. Two car doors slammed in the parking lot—one, then a moment later, the other. I listened for footfalls or keys turning in locks but heard nothing but the crashing surf outside. From the bed, I could see stars. At first, only the big ones: bright and fat and alone, jumping with urgency; and then the rest: tiny and fierce, a billion grains of sand spilling across the night sky, shining like the coast of heaven. Kelly's sleeping body rose and fell with each breath. I curled closer, held tighter. I pressed my nose to her back and through the thin cotton smelled the motel soap on her skin. Waves collapsed and exploded on the beach, one after the other, again and again. I was home.

George

My son Robert got married this year. He and his wife, Joy, called me from their honeymoon in Big Sur, California, to let me know they'd gone to city hall in Oakland to say their vows. Do I wish I'd been there? Of course I do. But it's how they wanted to go about things and it's their business. I was glad for the phone call. Joy is a strong woman and I think the two of them make sense together. They're not exactly what you'd call an affectionate couple or terribly expressive, or at least not from what I've seen in the few times I've seen them together. But given what Robert's been through, just making sense is more than adequate. They're both journalists, both busy, both black, both sober, and neither wants children. Robert writes about human rights abuses in government prisons, and Joy is obsessed with the impact of oil pipelines on indigenous lands. She spends a lot of time in Canada. When they talk about what they're working on, they both tend to shout, so when we speak on the phone or see each other, neither of which is often, I try to steer the conversation to safe subjects like the weather and pets. I love Robert and I know he loves me, but since his mother died over a decade ago, he's stayed away from Atlanta, his sisters, and me. For instance, his sisters haven't met Joy yet and they've been together for over four years. They don't make a fuss about it. Robert for them has always been less a brother and more like a cousin or young uncle who visits occasionally. Boarding school in Connecticut, five months in hospitals, two years of rehab and aftercare in Minnesota, and eventually college in Portland kept him away, sometimes even during Christmas. They knew a lot about him—he was so much and so often the subject of dinner-table talk in our house—but I don't think they ever had a chance to know him.

Robert was a fussy toddler. Easily upset, quick to cry. After kindergarten he calmed down and became quiet. Smart as hell and skipped the fourth grade, but he never appeared comfortable in his own skin. Didn't make friends easily. He had one friend from the neighborhood, Tim, a chubby, redheaded boy whom he played Dungeons & Dragons with and wrote adventure stories for, which Tim would illustrate with complicated pictures of four-armed, sword-wielding soldiers and magic fairies with no eyes. Robert never liked to share with us the little books they made. Kay and I would sneak peeks from time to time when Robert was in the bath just to check what was going on. Mostly the stories and pictures were pure fantasy. Occasionally you'd see something upsetting that suggested what our old family therapist would call displaced anger. I'm thinking now of the twin monkeys who got their heads snapped off by a flying griffin with an enormous beak. If the visual symbolism wasn't obvious enough, Robert's story described the death of the twin monkeys as necessary for the survival of the human race. That they would eat all Time, and without killing them the world would run out of hours. Impressive on the one hand for a ten-year-old, but especially disturbing since his room was across the hall from his twin sisters, who from their premature birth required lots of developmental and physical therapy and who ate up a lot of, well, time. Still, as rattled as I remember us being by that particular story, I don't remember talking to Robert about it, at the time, anyway; or discussing with him any of the books he and Tim made. I'm sure we should have, just as I'm sure we should have done many other things differently. But I think we were grateful he had a friend in Tim, creepy and aloof as he might be. Together, they had a sneaky air about them, and they'd spend hours in each other's room scribbling away and talking in a kind of code that Kay and I could never crack. Maybe all that sneakiness and escapism should have been a sign of what would happen later with Robert, but as a parent you just have no idea what anything means. On some level everything your kids do and say is in code. I'm sure some parents are expert at translating, but with Robert we didn't know where to begin. Also, we had a lot of other things to focus on at that time. The girls needed attention, and when they were three, Kay was diagnosed with stage-three breast cancer. Robert was ten then and often left alone to fend for himself. Between the girls and chemo appointments and trying to keep afloat the real estate development business my brother and I owned, there wasn't a lot of time to play basketball or go over home-work assignments. The funny thing is that Robert was the one person, the one area of our lives, we didn't worry about. He was so tidy and bright, so self-contained and quiet, that I assumed he didn't need me as much as everyone else did. Sure he had a spooky side, but he never got in any trouble. I was putting out a lot of fires then, and because with him there was no smoke, no flame, no alarms, I wasn't paying attention. Nothing that wasn't on fire got much of my time, which was something he must have understood from an early age. For the most part, I took him for granted. That he would shower and brush his teeth in the morning, get dressed and pour his own bowl of cereal. You'd think I would have been grateful to have a self-sufficient kid. I think for the most part I was. But a few times he drove me crazy. I remember one morning loading the girls into their car seats while Kay sat in the front sobbing from a migraine brought on by the chemo. The girls were fidgeting and whining and making it impossible to buckle their seat belts. We were late for school, for Kay's doctor's appointment, and at the time my brother was threatening to sell his half of the business if I didn't *get in the game,* as he put it. At the edge of all this sat Robert, cross-legged on the front step of the house, scribbling in his black-and-white composition book, writing one of those wild stories with fire-breathing turtles and dusty witches, completely oblivious to what was going on. I remember looking at him and feeling furious that he was exempt from responsibility, untouched by struggle. This is, of course, what you are supposed to want for your children, but in that moment it seemed unfair. What I wanted was to hit him, shake him violently, rattle his calm, and inflict some of what I was experiencing. It sounds insane, but a part of me felt that if I went near him in that moment, I might kill him. That's how angry I was. I couldn't stand it that nothing seemed to register with him, and I could not have been more wrong.

We sent Robert to boarding school when he was fifteen, which was when Kay's cancer came back and had spread to her lymph nodes. This time it was stage four and we panicked. The girls were eight by then and we reasoned that if Robert could focus on high school away from the chaos, it would be better for him. He had few friends, and Tim had left for Harkness the year before. Robert wanted to go, too, but at the time we didn't take the idea seriously. It was expensive and in the hills of Connecticut, where none of us had ever been. But a year later we felt under siege. We told ourselves it was what he wanted, and on some level by then I think we trusted his instincts about how he should be raised better than our own, so we said yes. What we didn't know was that by that time Tim had become quite the little drug czar at Harkness. I don't blame Tim, though for a long time I did. I've since learned that addicts are born, not made, so if it wasn't coke and heroin at Harkness, it might have been liquor and pills in Atlanta. Who knows. What I do know is that when I got the phone call from the headmaster at Harkness telling me that Robert had overdosed on drugs and was in a coma at the local hospital, I thought it was a joke. I'd never seen my son smoke a cigarette or even sip a beer. He was a straight-A student and played trumpet in the school marching band. He was a homebody and scarcely made a peep. The headmaster walked me through the prior twenty-four hours—a hiking trip that Tim and Robert and another student did not return from, a search party, a woman calling the police when she heard voices in her barn, and finding Robert unconscious when they arrived and the two other boys running away down the back field. *You need to come right away,* the headmaster said, and so I did.

After I landed in Hartford, checked into the motel in Wells, and visited Robert at the hospital, I saw clearly that the situation could change at any moment. My sister and mother moved in with Kay and the girls, and we agreed I should stay put until, hopefully, Robert could be moved— back home or to a rehab somewhere. I was out of my mind. I remember that strange little motel— with a girl's name, the Betsy—with bad art on the walls and orange Dial soap in the shower and by the sink. Not the little motel-size soaps, but the big, thick ones you buy in a grocery store. Something about that place was makeshift; definitely not a chain motel. It was clean and quiet and I spent the first two weeks coming back at night from the hospital and wondering how on earth I'd ended up in this room with flowers painted on the headboard and my son in a coma on the other side of this white, Norman Rockwell Connecticut town. Not until after Robert came out of the coma and was eventually moved from the ICU to the rehab unit did I see that motel room in daylight. This was when I met Lydia.

Dale

There is always one who goes away. This is what Mimi first said when Will sat us down his junior year in high school to tell us he wanted to go to college on the East Coast. His sister went to Reed, which felt like a world away, and his brother went to the University of Puget Sound in Tacoma. Both were within driving distance of Moclips, where we lived and raised our family: one north, one south. It was selfish of us, but we'd hoped Will would do the same. Don't get me wrong: we wanted them to go where they wanted to go, but our kids have been our life for the last two decades—we've been a team—and the change is hard. Both Mimi and I are only children and had parents who died young, so our kids are it. Maybe we just got lucky. Our kids were always great, better company even in their teens than most adults we know. Maybe it sounds unhealthy, or codependent, but it's true. Will's sister, Pru, took an interest in gardening when she was nine and inspired all of us to start seeding vegetables and herbs in the winter to plant in the spring. She organized a system of mulching that Mimi and I still follow to the letter today. By the time Pru left for college every one of us could have showed up on an organic farm anywhere ready to go to work. And Mike, Will's older brother, he's been turning us on to all kinds of new music since he was in the third grade. Through Mike we started listening to indie singer-songwriters like Ray LaMontagne and Cat Power. Through Mike we first heard Moby and then later Phoenix and Daft Punk. He also introduced us to the music of our own generation, which we for the most part missed: Sex Pistols, Kate Bush, Joy Division, Blondie. Lately he's fixated on eighties metal bands like AC/DC and Def Leppard, and that's where we part ways. And Will, he was more alert to what was happening politically and socially in the world than any of us. From an early age he was committed to the environment, the homeless. Later, he became obsessed with Rachel Corrie, the activist from Olympia who was killed by an IDF bulldozer while protesting the demolition of Palestinian homes. He followed every beat of that story: after she was killed the censorship in New York of the play based on her writings, the stone-walling of the US Congress to block an investigation into her death. Will was fourteen and writing letters to our congressman, letters of support to the Corrie family, insisting our whole family attend the rallies and memorials in her honor. He was a committed kid. He marched, he sat in, he sang, he organized. And we joined him. Neither Mimi nor I had ever been terribly political, but with Will he just brought these issues to life, and his sense of urgency and injustice and responsibility was infectious. His brother and sister teased him a little, but before they left for college, and even after, they showed up to nearly everything he asked them to. They were even arrested with Will when they chained themselves to a homeless shelter in Olympia that was scheduled for demolition due to budget cuts and a plan to develop the land where it stood. Mimi and I got the call from Mike, and we dropped everything right away to bail them out. We were not angry with them or disappointed. Just the opposite. The three of them chained to each other in support of something they believed in was evidence to us that, as parents, we'd done some-thing right.

So when Will told us he wanted to go to Amherst College, we were speechless. Tucked away in the hills of Massachusetts, the school might as well have been on Mars as far as we were concerned. Still, Will broke it to us sweetly, and the three of us cried and decided to call his sister and brother together to give them the news. It was the last year we lived in the house in Moclips. When Will left for college, we sold it to a couple who taught at the college in Aberdeen. They were newly married and planning a family, and what better fit could we have found. As teachers our-selves, elementary school, not college, we thought it was a good omen. We had bought the place from a widow who had never had children with her husband, but from what we gathered over the years, they'd been a tight pair, good people. We would still see her all the time, walking the road between the Moonstone where she worked and her sister's place, but Cissy was never much for small talk. We thought she was on the rude side of things when we first met her. We imagined that maybe she was holding a grudge against the young family who barged into her home and took over, but once we got to know Cissy, we began to understand that this was just her way. She didn't have a lot to say. After we moved in, she still came around, flipped the fuse switch when the power blew, jiggled the toilet just so when it wouldn't flush, even would bring overflow of firewood and kindling from her place to our porch in the winters. The one time I tried to pay her for cleaning the gutters she turned her back to me and walked away.

As a kid, Will was mesmerized by Cissy. It's understandable: she was over six feet tall and had a long, black braid with silver streaks the size of an anaconda. For a little guy she was an absolute giant. The summer we moved in, Will offered to help her clean the rooms at the Moonstone, and she said sure. He'd asked our permission and we just expected she'd say no, but when he came back from across the road and said he'd be back in a few hours, we couldn't go back on our word.

She paid him a buck each day. He was ten years old, scrubbing toilets and making beds and hauling garbage. Of course he soon began to give us cleaning lessons. Among other things, he showed us the secret to creasing hospital corners when making a bed and how to fold and hang towels properly. We'd ask him what he and Cissy talked about. *Oh, nothing,* he'd say. *Cissy doesn't talk.* Funny that a restless kid like Will never got impatient with that silence of hers. He was precocious, a talkative boy full of questions and opinions. To be honest, it's impossible to imagine the two of them in the Moonstone rooms—him emptying wastepaper baskets and putting new rolls of toilet paper in the dispensers and Cissy scrubbing the tubs and vacuuming. But the two were quite a pair, and it lasted on and off until the summer Will turned thirteen, when he began to become interested in the Quinault, the Native American tribe that had an active and large reservation up the beach. After that summer, he spent most of his time getting involved in any way he could on the reservation. He did anything they asked. He scraped and painted garages, the canoe sheds, their houses. A guy there named Joe Chenois, an elder, took a shine to Will and told him he'd spend one hour teaching him canoe carving for every week he worked on the reservation. Joe led Will to be interested in the law. Joe had been instrumental in the eighties in leading the fight to reclaim thousands of acres of Quinault land. He wasn't a lawyer, but he was an organizer and an activist, a leader, and he became expert in Native American laws, and the Constitution as it pertained to tribal sovereignty. Joe was Will's hero, and when he died of lung cancer in the fall of Will's freshman year in college, Will flew back to Seattle and drove down the coast to the memorial. We'd sold the house by then and it was the first time Will would stay at the Moonstone as a guest. Moonstone Beach, Moclips, and the history of the area was always more important to Will than it was to the rest of us. He'd read books on the massacres and the government land steals and tell us the stories with tears in his eyes. On the reservation they called him Little Cedar, a name Joe gave him the year Will carved his first and only canoe.

Lolly Reid was not the kind of girl we expected Will to fall for. We always thought he'd team up with the kind of girls he dated in high school. Outdoorsy, political girls. Earnest girls who were often pretty but unpolished. As disorganized and flighty as Lolly could be, she was polished. More beautiful than pretty. She had long blond hair and was stylish in a New York City kind of way. She read books but not about Indian massacres or fracking in the Catskills. She read novels, modern ones about families and secrets and love.

She spoke French and Italian and knew a lot about contemporary art from her mother, who ran galleries in New York and London. After college, Lolly worked in the photo department of a fashion magazine in New York. She was sophisticated culturally but not politically and was the kind of girl who, we thought, was invisible to Will. They met on a study-abroad program in Mexico sponsored by Vassar the spring semester of their junior year. Will went to Mexico because he was fascinated by the government's stewardship of the Mayan tribal culture, and he also wanted to refine his Spanish so that he could be a bilingual public defender. Lolly, on the other hand, decided at the last minute to follow her previous boyfriend into the program, but broke up with him a few days after they arrived, after she met our son. She explained this to us the night we met her, at a small restaurant she and Will liked to go to near their campus in Mexico City.

Who knows what draws people together? Lolly seemed unformed to us. Young. She was colorful and chatty, full of stories, but had few questions. She drew you in, but once you were there, you sensed she could vanish without warning. She had a way of telling two stories at once, looking behind you when she spoke. She seemed like someone who covered her bases, kept several balls in the air so she always knew she would have at least one in hand at the end of the day. She was clever, but not careful. She was, we recognized immediately, someone who could hurt our son. Around Lolly he was fatherly, patient, mesmerized. We watched him sweep up tortilla crumbs that had fallen down and around the table in front of her during the meal. He did this not once but three times, and as he did, she continued to talk, animate what she was saying with expressive eyes, passionate tones, and wild hand gestures, all the while absentmindedly spilling crumbs as she took bites of her food between words. Five months after that dinner, from the Moonstone in Moclips, he called to tell us he had proposed.

Lolly was the new Cissy, the new Joe Chenois, the new cause, the new Amherst. She was some-where Mimi and Pru and Mike and I had not been and could not go. Will always had that knack for frontiers, even if they were in our own backyard. But marrying Lolly felt different, risky and final at the same time.

They both still had their senior years to finish and I'm ashamed to admit that Mimi and I hoped the distance between Amherst and Vassar would be far enough to make their engagement seem like a summer folly. It is true we never got to know her well. Pru spent a week with her before the wedding. She asked Will if it would be okay. She'd only met Lolly twice before, and she said she just wanted to be with them, help in whatever way she could. Pru called us each of those days before we flew East for the wedding. She said she was beginning to understand Will's connection with Lolly. Twice we patched Mike in on these phone calls. It was like we'd sent an explorer to the new world and we hung on every word she used to describe what she saw and heard and how she felt. She described the old stone farmhouse where June and her boyfriend lived, the wide fields behind the house and the acres of trails on the Unification Church land, which their property bordered. She described everyone: June's boyfriend, Luke, who was much younger and, she said, beautiful. His mother, Lydia, who was hard to get to know, a bit standoffish but not in an arrogant way, more like a hurt animal would be. And June, who she said reminded her of Will: strong, competent, organized, but, like Will, a little undone around Lolly, deferential, in awe.

I remember the last call Pru made from that house. It was the night before we flew East. She would be joining us at the Betsy Motel once we arrived. Lolly's father was arriving in the morning, she told us, and there had been a fuss about where he was staying. Lolly had insisted he sleep at the house with them, and June, that afternoon, asked her to reconsider. It led to a big fight and Lolly of course won. But before it was over, it got heated and Pru went for a walk to clear her head and get a little distance from the tension. Later, on the way back to the house, she said she found June sitting on a fallen tree in the woods with her arms holding her sides, gently rocking. Pru didn't want to alarm her but it was too late to walk away. When June saw her, she waved her over and wiped the tears from her face. Pru asked if she was okay, and June answered with a question that seemed to Pru more of a comment on June's struggles with Lolly: *Did you ever have a family?* Pru said she sounded completely wiped out, at wit's end. She asked June if she wanted to walk back with her to the house, but she politely declined, saying she needed to be alone a little while longer.

Pru told us that night that she'd never felt as grateful. That her answer to June's question had been yes, but not as a commiseration, or an explanation of fatigue, as it seemed to be for June, but both as an acknowledgment of great fortune and a prayer of thanks. With Mike on the line from Tacoma, and Mimi and I huddled over her iPhone on speaker in the kitchen, Pru whispered to us, *Thank you.*

Kelly

It's a relief to finally find where you're meant to be. I always thought it was Seattle. I was born there. I grew up there. I met Rebecca and lived with her there for more than fiftcen years. I never questioned where I was supposed to be, but from time to time I got curious. Or maybe I was just restless for something new. I remember reading up on Provincetown, Massachusetts, in the year or so before I met Rebecca. Never got there, but it looked like a place to live. I even made a few phone calls about hotel jobs, but aside from summer business there isn't much in the way of hotel management. Holiday Inn had been good to me, and, thcn, it was unimaginable to leave Seattle for a job that wasn't with them. The nearest they had on the Cape was almost an hour from Provincetown, closer to Boston, which was no place that interested me. It always seemed to me like an East Coast Seattle but with more colleges and universities. Acres of Irish in both places, which is what I am and whom I'm from.

Few people are from where we are now. Moclips has less than two hundrcd ycar-round residents, and one way or another Cissy's family is related to most all of them. Not that Cissy has ever told us a thing about any of them, or herself. Whatever

137

we know about her we've pieced together from her sisters, who clammed up quick, or folks in Aberdeen, who are not exactly what you'd call loose-lipped, especially about one of their own to a couple of city dykes who will always—no matter how long we're here—be outsiders. Cissy is either a mystery or the opposite. All shadow or light. Either way, she lets us know what she wants known, and the rest is none of our business. She goes her way, we go ours, and we coexist as employer and employee.

Still, every so often she'll surprise you. Like a few months ago, when a film crew from a cable show set up cameras just down from the Moonstone. It was quite a production. They ran cords from generators in our parking lot out to the beach and parked a food truck alongside the road to feed the cast and crew. For days they filmed underwater divers walking in and out of the surf and shot footage of actresses dressed in mermaid costumes fanning their rubber tails in the waves. There were five girls, all young. Late teens, early twenties, and they stood shivering in bathrobes between takes, chain-smoking. On one of the nights things got rowdy in Room 5. The crew guys and the actresses were whooping it up, and we got calls not only from the guests in one of the two rooms not occupied by people from the TV show, but from the Sweeneys, the retired couple who live next door, who have never once complained to us. It was just past ten at night when they called. Rebecca and I were watching an episode of some British series on DVD, so I hit pause, put on my boots and coat, grabbed my flashlight, and headed for where the noise was coming from. I could smell the pot smoke long before I reached the door and hear the loud reggae music broken by the occasional burst of screaming laughter. As I approached the door, I could see the door to Room 6 open. I expected Jane to appear, but instead it was Cissy, wearing her Carhartt canvas jacket buttoned to the top and her long silver braid tucked inside. Someone who didn't know her might have seen a tall, stern-looking man emerge from the door of one motel room and step quickly to the door of another. Cissy did not bother knocking but instead pulled out her master key and opened the door right up. I could hear her yell *OUT!* just the one time. Right away, the music stopped. I stepped back to the side of the building to watch. I don't know why, but I didn't want Cissy to see me. One by one the girls began to stumble out, some alone, others with guys from the crew. Eventually, everyone made it back to their rooms. Once Cissy was satisfied, she walked down the path toward the office, and turned left onto Pacific Avenue toward her sister's house. Had Jane called Cissy? Or had Cissy been in Jane's room when the racket started? I stood in the shadows of the motel building wondering whether to check in on Jane or call Cissy. Neither seemed right, so I walked toward the beach and watched the waves crash for a little while. The moon was not visible that night, so the only light came from the motel, the few houses along the beach, and farther down, where 109 cuts close to the sand, the dim and infrequent twitch of headlights. I tried to imagine how it was two hundred years ago, when only the Quinault tribe walked the beach. Cissy's sister Pam told us that this land was where the tribe brought their teenage girls to be safe after they reached puberty and before they married. Who guarded them? I wondered. Surely not men, the very thing the girls were being protected from. I wondered, too, how many of them never married, either by bad luck or by choice. Did they have a choice then? I doubted it. Did those women stay on and help protect the younger girls? Or were they sent back to the tribe at some unmarriageable age to live out the rest of their years as spinsters?

Local legend has it that one night all the sleeping girls were swallowed by the sea. Rebecca and I have heard at least half a dozen variations on the tale—one involves a sea witch who cast a spell, another a falling star that crashed into the ocean and caused a mighty tidal wave, and one starts with a terrible fire that drove the animals from the hills into the ocean, carrying the girls with them in the stampede. But in every version of the story, the sleeping girls end up underwater, where they somehow transform into mermaids, enchanted protectors whose magic keeps the Quinault virgins from harm. No doubt some scrap of this story must have made its way to the producers making the silly television show.

I walked toward the water to make out the shape of the waves in the pitch-black night. The wind was rough and I pulled my turtleneck up above my face just below my eyes. I stood a few feet from the surf and imagined the chain-smoking actresses as real-life mermaids, gorgeous and fierce, their scales shining. Who wouldn't want to be protected by such creatures? I thought of Penny and Rebecca, who looked after each other as kids and later, too, as adults. For most of their lives they only had each other. I always had older brothers and cousins and uncles, and even though my being gay was not anyone's first choice (including mine, initially), after I came out in high school anyone who made fun of me or worse was swiftly dealt with by my family. After a while, because they had to, the kids in my school accepted me. I wasn't prom queen or anything, but I was cocaptain of the field-hockey team, vice president of my senior class, and I organized a volunteer soup kitchen on the weekends my junior and senior years. What I'm saying is that I wasn't on my own. I felt different, unsure of how to make my way romantically, but I felt safe. My family gave me that, and the older I get, the more I see how lucky I was. All but one of my brothers moved East, my parents aren't around anymore, and I have one uncle in a nursing home in Olympia. Rebecca is my family now. She has me and I have her and it's where we belong.

Penny didn't have anyone the night she died. No mermaids, no Rebecca. Before that night on the beach, I had never considered just how alone Penny must have felt. How completely on her own in that danger she was. I turned back toward the Moonstone and started walking home. The only lights on now were from Room 6. Jane. Probably the most alone person I've ever met. I'd seen plenty of lonely travelers at the Holiday Inn in Seattle and even here, but no one like Jane, who seemed half in the world and half out of it. She has been, in the few times I've actually seen and spoken with her, nearly without life. Still, she has Cissy. How exactly, we do not know, but it is clear she has in her a formidable ally. I wonder if she sees it that way, is aware how far this stranger has taken her under her wing.

A few weeks after Jane checked in, Rebecca and I noticed that Cissy was coming and going from Room 6 just a little bit more than was usual. We then began to see her carrying around a giant green thermos, the kind you see on camping trips with a big silver, screw-off top that doubles as a bowl or cup depending on what's inside. We'd never seen her with it before, but not long after Jane checked in we saw that thermos in Cissy's hands most days. Rebecca and I eventually pieced together that she was dropping it off at Room 6 in the morning when she started cleaning the rooms and picking it up at the end of the day. At first, Jane would leave it outside the door on the cement stoop, but after a while we noticed that Cissy would step inside to pick it up—usually for only a minute or two but occasionally for longer.

This business with the thermos has been going on for over seven months. What those two could possibly speak about or have in common I can't imagine, and I'll admit at first it irked me to be excluded from whatever bond they'd developed, but now when I see Cissy heading to Room 6 with that giant green thermos, I just think, Thank God that sad woman pulled up to our motel, and not some other godforsaken place. Thank God she has someone to look out for her. Thank God any of us do.

Lydia

He's explained it all before and it still makes no sense. In that voice of his that rises and falls and swoops like a song. *You are a lucky lady, Lydia Morey. Lucky, indeed. This lottery you have won is over three million dollars and is only awarded once every two years.* At times she does not hear a word he is saying, just his voice. She has fallen asleep with the phone cradled between her ear and shoulder, his voice a lullaby, spinning tales of millions. The prize, he says, has never before been given to an American, and technically it cannot be, but Winton is offering to help her, putting himself on the line to steer her through the red tape so she can receive her money. *This,* he says with an ocean of warmth in his voice, *is what I will do for you.*

Sometimes she hangs up on him, leaves the receiver off the hook and turns out the light. But he always calls the next day. Usually between nine and ten in the morning and then again after six o'clock, after she's mailed her bills, shopped for her few groceries—toilet paper, cans of Progresso soup, English muffins—and had her coffee at the coffee shop. Often, when she is unlocking the door to the apartment, she hears the phone ringing. The few times it hasn't, she's been

144

disappointed. It's a scam and she knows it. He is flirtatious and personal, warm and bullying, and she understands that she is being drawn in, manipulated, made dependent. She knows all this but still she picks up the phone. Occasionally, like a teenager who tells her mother to tell the boy she has a crush on that she's not home when he calls, she will let it ring. But she will pick up the next day and she knows it. Winton knows it, too, because he always calls again. *Lydia Morey, I missed you yesterday. You must have been out cutting a rug or breaking some poor boy's heart.* After a month of the calls and the talk of prize money and red tape and risk, Winton begins to apply a little pressure, set a clock to the proceedings. The three million dollars will go to someone else if she does not pay the international prize taxes. The first tax is $750, pennies compared to what she will have, and it is a sum the prize committee reimburses. They would pay it directly for her but it is not allowed. She must pay first and then the committee will send her that amount right away. Paying this tax, Winton says without music, is necessary to continue.

She pays. She drives to Walmart in Torrington, puts $750 on a money card as Winton suggested, and mails it to an apartment in Astoria, Queens, where a designated representative from the lottery lives. Walmart, Queens, money cards, reimbursements—she is amazed he thinks she will believe any of it. And still she's not ready to step away. Not prepared just yet to come home in the evening each night knowing there will be no phone call. As well, there is also a thin, far-off hope that somehow the ludicrous scenario Winton has described is true. She has even allowed herself the fantasy of sending him money after she wins to pay for his schooling, to help him support his family. But it's all a farce and she knows it will expire or she will end it soon, but not just yet. So she allows herself to think of the $750 as a test. A test she knows he will fail, and because he will, the farce will end and all will return to being as it was. She deliberately does not think this through, actively protects herself from recognizing how wasteful this is. She will see this to its end and she does not ask herself why.

And so she puts the money card in an envelope addressed to Theodore Bennett in Astoria, Queens, the prize official Winton mentioned. Winton also told her there should be no note inside and no return address on the envelope. And though the idea of $750 floating out there without a return address is intolerable, she still complies and drops the untraceable envelope in the mailbox in front of the Town Hall.

In the days that follow, the calls from Winton continue and she settles back into their established routine. A morning call she mostly avoids, an evening call she takes. She listens to him talk about his last girlfriend, who cheated on him and left him crushed, the son she never lets him see, his sick mother, his sister in jail. His world blinks to life over these calls. He is a jilted boyfriend, a dutiful and worrying son. He is twenty-eight, he says. He is taking classes at night to get a degree in accounting so he can quit his job with the lottery, which pays poorly and is only part-time. He would have quit months ago but he'd like to steer this year's prize to Lydia before he goes. Just do this one last thing because he'd like to see a good woman like Lydia get the money. Not some European asshole, the type who usually takes the prize.

Over time his sister in jail becomes his cousin, his aunt, his niece. The class at night is for engineering, for hotel management, for graphic design. The girlfriend's name is Carla, Nancy, Tess, Gloria. He is twenty-eight, twenty-four, thirty. The inconsistencies alarm Lydia at first and then amuse. Further proof that she's right, that the whole thing is a hoax. But then Winton begins to ask again about her life. Questions he asked in the beginning but she deflected. Is she married, what does she do for work, does she have children? And now, because something else must begin on these phone calls for them to continue, she tells him about Earl Morey, her ex-husband. The redheaded boy who was a lot of fun and then none at all. Who called her Snacks and pinched her leg and butt and left small purple-and-yellow bruises. Who knocked her in the head with a phone book one night so hard it made her lose her balance the whole next day. Who stayed at the Tap with his brothers and cousins and uncles most nights and would come home drunk and, if she was lucky, sleep on the couch of their small apartment. She was nineteen and married, and within the year she hated him and his whole family and she could do nothing. When she finally confessed what was going on to her mother, she told her daughter to zip it and be grateful she'd found a man from a good family. She tells all this to Winton, and as she talks about this time, it's as if she's reading a bedtime story to her son when he was a boy, about a girl who made the wrong turn in the forest and had no way out. She talks and talks, just as Winton had in the beginning, and she hears him breathing on the other end of the phone. Only rarely does he ask a question or comment on anything she's said, and if he does, it is punctuation and no more. *What a fool, that stupid man,* he has said. *A drunken fool.* She does not mention other men, the ones who pursued her until they slept with her and then stopped calling. Nor does she mention Rex. And Luke, she says nothing about him.

Ten days after she mails the letter, a padded manila envelope with a Newark, New Jersey, postmark arrives, and in it are seven hundred-dollar bills and a fifty. No note, no paper of any kind. Just the money. Later that day, she tucks the roll of bills in the pocket of her fleece pullover and walks to the coffee shop. It is early February but Christmas decorations are still taped to the windows. They are the kind you buy at the drugstore or the supermarket: thin, cardboard Santas, plate-size snowflakes, Rudolph the Red-Nosed Reindeer. Along the ceiling and at the top of the windows are strung small, white lights, and on the counter by the register is a miniature artificial Christmas tree wrapped in a silver garland with a plastic angel on top. The money in Lydia's pocket gives her an unfamiliar energy, a lift. She knows it's hers, that she's been given nothing, won nothing, but still the large bills and the way they arrived give her a surge. She drinks her coffee quickly, and when the check comes, she pays with the fifty. The waitress, Amy, who now looks like she is well into her eighth month, picks up the bill and returns the change without comment or any evidence of interest. Lydia leaves a five-dollar tip, pulls on her fleece jacket, and starts home.

Before she reaches the sidewalk, she notices a boy in a green sweatshirt circle the parking lot on his bike and cross in front of her. She's seen him before. Hanging out on the green with his friends, smoking. He worked for Luke, but dozens of kids in Wells between the ages of thirteen and twenty-two worked for Luke at one time or another. What did June call them? Pickpockets and potheads? Lydia winces at the memory of June's teasing and watches the boy swoop in tight circles with his bike.

Could this be Kathleen Riley's boy? she wonders, and imagines what he's heard his mother spewing about her. Lydia reminds herself that Kathleen's name is no longer Riley, that it's been Moore for many years. Kathleen married a contractor from Kent who built her a big house on Wildey Road and was a nurse at the hospital before she started having kids. Funny, Lydia thinks, to think of Kathleen Riley as a nurse and a mother. Her sharpest memory of Kathleen is from high school, when she accused Lydia of stuffing her bra. Lydia was the first in her seventh-grade class to noticeably need a bra, and so by the time she entered high school she was more developed than any of the other girls her age. On the second day of high school she was given the nickname Lactadia. No one claimed credit for the name but it stuck, and soon the older boys were writing her lewd notes and slipping them into her locker, asking to go for a walk behind the bleachers at school, catcalling when she got on the bus. *I'm thirsty,* they'd yell from the backseat in the mornings, and in the afternoon from the open windows once she got off at the bus stop at the end of the town green. By the second week of school many of the girls in the higher grades, Kathleen Riley among them, took a fierce disliking to Lydia. Being younger than Kathleen by two years, Lydia had been invisible to her in elementary school. Now that they were in high school, Kathleen not only saw her, she waged war against her. *Lactadia has no milk* was her favorite chant, and in the stairwell once between classes she and her friends cornered Lydia. Kathleen demanded she lift her shirt to prove she wasn't stuffing her bra with tissues. Lydia was so frightened that instead of walking away or telling Kathleen to fuck off, she slowly lifted her blouse above her head and exposed her very real breasts. Lydia remembers standing there, shirt up, covering her face, hearing kids pass her on the stairs and one of them grabbing her right breast and squeezing it hard. She couldn't see whose hand it was and she was too stunned to respond. By the time she lowered her blouse, Kathleen and the others had turned away and were rushing down the stairs. Lydia could hear the word *freak* echo as they descended in a storm of cackling laughter. There were other humiliations, and thousands of half-heard whispers, but the memory of being exposed and mauled before the accusing eyes of Kathleen Riley and her friends is the most mortifying. Not until the older girls had graduated and Lydia began dating Earl, who was popular and feared and came with a force field of protection, did the terror she felt approaching school each day begin to lift. Now, every few weeks or so, Lydia will see Kathleen coming down the aisle at the grocery store or standing in line at the pharmacy, and when she does, she is always careful to keep her head down and avoid eye contact. As if they were still in high school, she gets out of the way, becomes invisible.

Lydia squints to get a better look at the boy on the bike though still can't be sure he's Kathleen's son. She's always known most people in town, but once Luke was out of school and later, after Rex left and she stopped going out to the Tap and places like it, she kept to herself and had little to do with anyone beyond those she worked for. Slowly, without noticing, she started losing track of the marriages and births, the breakups and new people. But this kid she's noticed. And lately, too often. She remembers one of her mother's kitchen-table wisdoms, which she'd typically trot out on the occasion of hearing some piece of local, fallen-from-grace gossip: *Good apples get picked, it's the rotten ones that fall close to the tree.* It never made sense to Lydia. It still doesn't, but it begins to as she watches up ahead, where the boy who is probably Kathleen Riley's son swerves off Main Street onto Low Road and disappears. Lydia walks faster and, in her coat pocket, crushes money in her fist.

Silas

He ditches his bike behind a garbage shed on Low Road and cuts back through the field behind the elementary school to Herrick Road. At first, she is out of sight, seven or eight driveways ahead, but soon he is close enough to see her arms swing at her sides, her jeans pockets ride the wild movement of her ass. It's been like this for months. She walks, he follows, closer and closer, narrowing the gap between them each time. Lately, he's been close enough to see the faint outline of panties and bra straps behind her clothes. He'd heard from someone that Luke's mom was in her fifties, but as he watches her ass rock back and forth and jiggle up and down in her tight jeans, he thinks, No fucking way. He's seen it in shorts, sweatpants, tight skirts, loose skirts, and many times and most often in jeans that look like these. Lydia Morey walks a lot. Mostly to the coffee shop, the bank, and the grocery store, and she walks as if she's stoned or in a trance of some kind. She never turns around, hardly ever looks to either side. He's pretty sure she has not seen him, even once, in the weeks and months that have passed since he started following her.

He rushes his pace to get closer. That ass! He's spellbound by the metronomic perfection of its movement—up-down, down-up—and thinks, This is no mom's ass. He winces, ashamed by his racing mind, regretting this particular thought. His gaze pulls back to take in the rest of her. He sees her hands, her ringless fingers, her wrists, her worn sneakers, the dark brown hair piled on her head tumbling in loose strands down around her shoulders. For the first time, he sees a few gray hairs. With these she becomes again a whole person, not just a few thrilling body parts. She returns to being the reason he parks his bike four doors down from her apartment on Upper Main Street in the mornings before work in the summer and on Saturdays now that school has started up again. She becomes, again, his dead boss's mom. Lydia Morey. The woman people in town talk about. The woman he's heard described as the mother of the crackhead whose negligence blew up a house and killed three people and himself; the sex-mad slut who cheated on Earl Morey with a migrant worker, a drug dealer, a hitchhiker, a Zulu tribesman; the mother of the hustler who conned June Reid into being his sugar mama until she threw him out and he came back on a suicide mission; the monster who gave birth to a bad seed who finally got what was coming to him. He's heard it all and has kept quiet every time. The only remotely nice thing he's ever heard said about Lydia Morey was that she had *the best rack in Litchfield County*. His father made the comment this summer as they waited at a stop sign in town and she crossed in front of them wearing a tan halter top. *Not even the young girls at the Tap can compete with that,* he added. Silas's mother, who never liked Lydia Morey, was not in the car. When her name was mentioned in their house, she was always quick to comment that Lydia was someone for whom she had *no use.* She also said, after getting off the phone with one of her friends a few days after everything happened, *I suppose no one ever told Lydia that when you lie down with dogs, you not only get fleas, you get pregnant with more dogs. How June Reid ever got mixed up with that mutt son of hers I'll never know.* Even through this Silas stayed silent.

The only time he ever spoke about any of it was when he was questioned by the police and the fire marshal about working at June Reid's the day before the wedding. They came to the door of his house that night and he sat in the kitchen and told them the same thing Ethan and Charlie told them. That Luke had them do what he usually had them do for New Yorkers like June Reid: pick up twigs and sticks, pull weeds from the sidewalk, and edge the flower beds. The only difference was that Luke paid everyone in advance that day and double their regular twelve bucks an hour. As he was handing out their cash, he asked them to do twice as good a job as usual.

You guys are good, but today I need great. Silas told the police officers that Luke had said this, but they didn't seem interested. They kept asking about Luke's mood, whether he seemed drunk or high or upset when they saw him last. Silas said he seemed like he always seemed. A little stressed-out, busy, but fine. He told them that he and the other guys showed up at June Reid's place around two that day, and Luke worked alongside them for the first couple hours. He rode the John Deere, mowing the front and back lawns, while Ethan, Charlie, and Silas did everything else. Around four o'clock, Luke said he had errands to run, so he left them to finish working until six thirty, after which Charlie and Ethan piled into Ethan's old Saab and Silas rode his bike down Indian Pond Road to his house, which was less than a mile away.

What none of them told the cops was that not long after Luke left, the three of them booked across the field behind the house to the trails that led to the Unification Church property, what kids in town called the Moon because, as everyone knew, the Unification Church was just another name for the Moonies. They did not say that they had sprinted to the Moon and took turns pulling from Silas's bong. They also did not say that it turned out all three had a stash, so they mixed a little from each into the bowl and smoked what Charlie called, sarcastically, *a wedding salad.*

They lost track of time on the Moon, and when they got back it was almost six. After Silas ditched his yellow knapsack inside the stone shed outside the kitchen, the three of them rushed through the rest of the work and left before dark. By then, the driveway was packed with cars and the house was full for the rehearsal dinner, so they took off without saying anything to Luke, who they assumed was pissed that they were nowhere to be seen when he returned. They also didn't want him to clock that they were high. Before leaving, Silas remembers, he saw Lydia inside the screened porch. She was sitting with June on the wicker sofa, laughing, small candles all around them flickering on tables holding flowers and food. He cannot remember anything more about seeing these two women, but he remembers clearly the sweet smell of freshly cut lawn, the sound of tent fabric slapping the air, and the first streaks of sunset painting the sky pink. These were the seconds before he left for home, and he has replayed each one a million times.

It is hard to believe the woman on the porch that night in May is the same one walking with grim purpose ahead of him now, bundled in a purple fleece, trudging across Herrick Road to Upper Main Street. Not once since that night has he seen her smile or heard her laugh.

Silas slows down to let a gap expand between

them. He wonders if Lydia even knows who he is. He'd worked for Luke on and off for three summers and on weekends in the fall and spring. He wonders if she saw him that day at June Reid's. He remembers standing by the stone shed and rushing away when he heard Luke's voice coming from the kitchen. He remembers running toward the driveway and flying on his bike along the green cornfields that stretch from the edge of June Reid's property past the church where June's daughter was getting married the next day. He slowed down when he came upon Indian Pond, reflecting the red-and-purple sunset stretching above him. He remembers fireflies blinking from the brush and woods on both sides of the road as he pedaled. He remembers stopping to crawl down the rocky slope to the water's edge to take a leak, the wild sky and the surface of the pond still as glass until his piss sent it rippling. The effect was trippy and especially so since he was still high. At one point the clouds shifted and above him spread what looked like a great dragon with wings as wide as the world. Silas stumbled back from the lake as the creature came into view: jaws jagged with teeth and blasting fire, smoke curling from its snout, magnificent wings expanding in scales of cloud, its gigantic tail twisting past the horizon. It was a spectacular beast, its eyes the only visible blue, long slits that appeared to widen as its head turned slowly toward Silas where he sat against the bank, dazzled and afraid.

All these months later, he had forgotten about the dragon and how, for a few terrifying seconds, he believed it was real. He'd forgotten that it was dark by the time he found his way up the bank to the road, and how at first he could not find his bike. He thinks about those moments when he stumbled in the dark before finding his bike, which had fallen down next to the tree he'd leaned it against earlier. He wishes he could return to that stumbling. To that perfectly blind minute before he knew anything. Not where his bike was. Not what would happen later that night, or the next morning. Not that a full moon would soon rise and light the whole valley. Or that later, after everyone in his family had gone to sleep, he'd scramble back onto his bike to pedal furiously down this same road, counting on the light of the moon to guide his way to June Reid's house.

Without noticing, he has quickened his pace and closed the gap between him and Lydia. After crossing Herrick onto the sidewalk that runs the length of Upper Main Street, he forgets he's supposed to remain hidden. What had only minutes before been at least three or four car lengths has now collapsed to only a few yards. When he realizes how close he is, he knows he should slow his pace to a quiet halt and bank left down one of the driveways out of sight. But he's never been this close before. He thinks he can hear her breathing. The air is cold, but he can see perspiration beading on the back of her neck. She has taken off her fleece and he can see patches of skin through the sweat-soaked cloth of her white T-shirt. His eyes move from one patch of almost exposed skin to another. He leans closer. His shoe scuffs the pavement, scrapes loudly against the loose sand, and for the first time he can see her register his presence. His other foot accidently kicks a twig that hits the back of her ankle and she stops abruptly, turns around. He freezes. She is inches away.

June

After the maze of rock-strewn, erosion-destroyed dirt roads leading away from Bowman Lake, the smooth asphalt of Route 93 south of Kalispell is a relief. When she sees the sign for Butte, she drifts toward the exit for Interstate 90 and, later, takes another exit when she sees the sign for Salt Lake City. A few miles into Idaho she can feel the wagon pulling to the left. It gets worse, so she gets off at the next exit, and by the time she finds a Texaco she can barely keep the car moving in a straight line. The kids at the register have no idea how to change a tire. The place is more of a grocery store that happens to sell gas than a gas station where anyone knows anything about cars. She waits for someone to pull in who looks like they know what to do. Soon, an older guy with a thick head of white hair and closely trimmed beard, wearing a red flannel shirt, backs his truck up to a pump. When she asks him if he knows how to change a tire, the amused look on his face makes it clear she's picked the right guy. He puts out his hand and says, *Brody Cook reporting for duty.* She shakes his hand but says nothing. *All right then,* he says, still cheerful. He smiles and finishes pumping and paying for his gas. After he pulls his truck away from the pumps and parks next to the Subaru, he asks where she keeps the spare and she says she isn't sure the wagon has one. *One of two places,* he says, *heads or tails?* He looks at her expectantly and she has no idea how to respond. *Okay, let's try heads.* He pops the hood and after one quick look around the engine says, *Tails it is.* When he steps to the back of the wagon and opens the hatch, she hears him ask where she'd like him to put the bags. He asks again. When she doesn't answer, he walks around the car with a suitcase in one hand and a duffel bag in the other and puts them down on the asphalt. *I'll leave you in charge of these,* he says before returning to extract the spare tire from under the panel beneath the rug.

They had been with her all along. Shoved in the back of the Subaru, packed and ready and forgotten. Is it possible, she wonders, that she hasn't opened the hatch since she started driving? She's had no reason to go back there. She brought nothing with her, acquired nothing on the way besides the toothbrush and paste she picked up at a gas station in Pennsylvania the first day. How long has it been? A week? Two? She lost track of time almost as soon as she left Connecticut. Even now she can't remember how many nights she slept in the wagon next to Bowman Lake. Three nights? Four? She stayed until the bottles of water and bags of peanuts and raisins she'd stocked up on in Ohio ran out. However long she's been on the road, these bags have been with her the whole time.

It is obvious who belonged to each one. Will's is a sleek arrangement of zippers and pockets with wheels and collapsible handle; Lolly's is a frayed olive canvas duffel with taped leather straps and ink stains. Lolly would never have been so organized as to pack everything the night before and have the bags waiting in the car. This was Will's handiwork. Will was the son-in-law Adam always dreamed of: the kind of guy to read up on infectious diseases in foreign countries before traveling there, who paid all of his bills on time, filled the coffeemaker with water and ground beans and set the timer the night before. The kind of guy to make sure the bags for his honeymoon in Greece were packed and waiting in his mother-in-law's car the night before his wedding. June can hear him walking Lolly through the schedule. Wedding at one, reception from two to six, out the door and in June's car by seven so that June and Luke would get them to Kennedy Airport no later than 9:30 for their 11:45 flight to Athens. He even e-mailed the itinerary to Lolly, Adam, his parents, and Luke and June so that no one was unclear when everything needed to occur.

Lolly's duffel is only half zippered, and at one end, sticking out just a few inches, June sees the edge of a pale blue towel. Brody turns the jack to raise the front left corner of the car, and she feels like walking away. From him, the car, the bags, the towel. As she steps back, quietly, one foot slowly behind the other, she hears Lolly calling to Will, *Wait! I forgot my vitamins!* This is after the rehearsal, after the dinner, after Luke has cleaned up the mess from making chili for everyone. After Adam has gone to bed and Lydia, a little tipsy, has gone home. June is at the kitchen table sorting neglected piles of mail. *Wait!* Lolly calls from her room after Will is already out the front door with the bags. She slams down the back stairs like she always has—loud and fast and sounding like an avalanche. She flies out the door in bare feet clutching in both hands a light blue towel from the upstairs bathroom she's made into a makeshift satchel for her bottles of vitamins. *Come back! I have no shoes!* June hears them laughing just outside the house and thinks, with a loose knot of nostalgia and envy, that this moment in their relationship, in their lives, is as good as it will ever get. The before. *The top of the Ferris wheel,* a man she went on a date with in London once told her as they rode above the city in the newly opened Eye. This blind date was arranged by a pushy but well-intentioned colleague at the gallery. The man was her colleague's uncle and a widower, and for both of them it was too soon. Most of that evening has faded from memory, but when they reached the top of the great wheel and saw the golden lights of London fan out in gorgeous chaos below, she remembers him explaining his theory with an exhausted patience she had gotten used to in English men. *This is the pivot between youth and age, the thrilling place where everything seems visible, feels possible, where plans are made. On the one side you have childhood and adolescence, which are the murky ascent, and, on the other, you have the decline that is adulthood, old age, the inch-by-inch reckoning of that grand, brief vision with earthbound reality.*

Listening to Lolly and Will whisper and giggle outside, she imagines them swinging in a golden seat atop a Ferris wheel. She lets the image linger. She has not opened any of the mail spread out before her on the table. She pictures London that night, a maze of light stretching glamorously in every direction. She sees Lolly there, above it all, laughing. She pushes around the bills and letters, absentmindedly arranging them by shape and color. Then she hears Lolly, calling to her from the still-open front door to come and unlock the wagon. It is chilly and she puts her linen jacket on and, when she does, feels in the left pocket the card Luke borrowed earlier to get cash to pay the kids he'd hired to fix up the lawn. She grabs the keys from the brass tray she usually tosses them in and goes out to the driveway to open the car for Will. When they return, Lolly is barefoot on the front mat in her ratty sweatpants, elegant blouse still on from the evening, waiting for the two of them to come back inside. She is laughing her goofy laugh. When she sees June in the flood-light beams in front of the house, she calls out *Mom!* ridiculously, without thinking, like a teenager with an easy relationship with her mother. The top of the Ferris wheel is a giddy and thoughtless place, June thinks, and so briefly enjoyed. When she gets to the front step, she hugs her daughter for as long as she will let her.

They go inside and Luke makes chamomile tea. The four of them sit on the screened porch talking about the rehearsal earlier and the chili and deviled-egg dinner. Will is teasing Lolly about being late to the church the next day, losing the ring, and flubbing her vows. Feeling unusually playful with Lolly, June chimes in about how as a kid she'd been in the bathroom when she was meant to make her one, brief appearance in *Babes in Toyland*, the school play in eighth grade. The talk is jolly, the teasing gentle, but gradually Lolly becomes quiet, as if she's suddenly realized she's dropped her guard and forgotten to maintain a safe distance. She recedes, and the talk moves on to Will's upcoming second year in law school, what he'll do once he's graduated—internships, clerkships, jobs. After a while and out of nowhere, Lolly asks

Luke if he is going to ask her mother to marry him. All talk stops. No jest is in her voice, no play at all. Luke meets her eyes and her tone. *I have. But your mother doesn't take the question seriously. Or me seriously. Hard to tell which. At first I thought she blew it off because of you, but now that you're older and out of college and practically married, I'm beginning to wonder. Lately I've been hoping all this wedding stuff would rub off on her, but it hasn't. So the answer to your question is yes, and the answer to mine, asked twice, is no.* This isn't the response Lolly expects. No one does, including, by the look on his face, Luke. The only sound is the dishwasher humming in the kitchen and the impenetrable sound of the cicadas, which has graduated from an electric buzz to a droning roar. After a few uncomfortable seconds, Lolly stands and pulls Will with her. They leave the porch as Will apologetically says good night for both of them. *See you in the morning,* he calls from the top of the stairs, before Lolly's bedroom door slams shut. They are gone.

A long flatbed stacked high with sheets of plywood bangs loudly by. June is walking against traffic, head down, past the Arby's, the Taco Bell, the Exxon. She sees Luke's shoes, the brown, buckled ones he bought from one of her mail-order catalogs just for the wedding. They are shined perfectly, but on them she can see drops of tomato that must have fallen when he was cooking dinner. Tiny thatches of freshly mown grass whisker from the edges of the soles. A small clump falls on the bluestone as Luke nervously kicks at the leg of the wicker coffee table. Neither has spoken since Lolly and Will went upstairs to bed. Luke continues to fidget and she can see white gym socks peeking out from his khaki trousers. His hand moves to her leg, his thumb begins to rub her thigh before she pushes it off and gets up to leave. He reaches for her hand, and in smacking it away, she grazes his cheek with her nail just below his left eye. He winces and pulls away. She does not apologize, does not stop to see if she's drawn blood, does not hesitate as she steps from the porch into the kitchen.

Over the sound of passing cars, she hears someone calling. *Lady! LADY!!!* She knows she should stop but the feeling is far away.

She is at the sink filling the kettle with water to boil for more chamomile tea. Her hands are shaking. She wishes she could return to how it was earlier in the day. Everything until now had gone on without incident. Even with Adam, who arrived in the morning from Boston, alone and without a girl, thank God. June had at the last minute tried to persuade Lolly how much easier it would be on everyone if he stayed at the Betsy, where Will's family and others were staying, but her response was instant and volcanic, and despite June's delicate approach and stated worries, Adam was installed in the guest bedroom upstairs. Still, he'd been friendly to Luke, which was out of character and surprising given how he'd behaved when they met last year at Lolly's graduation from Vassar. Adam refused to acknowledge Luke, and all afternoon muttered *cradle robber* and *cougar* under his breath. Regrettably, June responded on his level and reminded Adam that he'd been raiding the nursery long before their marriage was over. She remembers how quiet Luke became and how only later that night did she see the afternoon through his eyes: two middle-aged, bitter exes pointing fingers at each other for dating younger people. It was humiliating. She swore she'd avoid this kind of squabbling at Lolly's wedding, and to her surprise, so far, it had required no effort. Adam had been respectful. No barbs, no bite. The last person she expected to upset the applecart was Luke. But by letting Lolly rattle him as he had, he'd opened up a can of worms she believed, or at least hoped, had been closed.

The kettle is full but she can't move it from beneath the faucet. It is overflowing, but the gushing water, the weight of it in her hand, is soothing. She has no idea what to do next, so she does nothing. She feels cornered and angry and wrong. She wishes she could return to the front walk just an hour or so ago, hear Lolly call to her when she saw her step into the beams of the floodlights. *Mom!* She wishes she could start the evening over from there, steer it away from where it is. She watches the steady flow of water from the faucet, how it spills from the top of the kettle and disappears down the drain.

Cars whiz by, horns wail. She is walking faster, but the voice is closer. *LADY! What on earth?!?* She begins to run and soon someone grabs her arm. *STOP,* the voice shouts. *What the hell are you doing?* it asks, more bewildered than angry. She looks at the source—the beard, the flannel shirt, the white head of hair—but she does not see the man who helped her earlier. *I'm sorry,* she says, but not to this man. She is looking at the loose water, her trembling hands. *Oh, God, I'm so sorry,* she says again, dropping to one knee and then the other. For the first time, far enough away and next to someone she does not know, she cries.

George

I'd leave in the morning and the room would be a mess—sheets and blankets twisted in knots, clothes and towels on the floor. But when I'd come back at night after a day at the hospital with Robert, the place would be impeccable. The bed made, my clothes neatly folded on the dresser. Even the cap on my toothpaste would be screwed back on and my razor and comb lined up neatly on a folded face towel next to the sink. I'm not a messy person, normally, but when I look back on my time at the Betsy, I can see that I let myself slip. I had lost control of everything—my wife's health, my boy, my business—and in this one space, this little New England motel room, the problems that existed could be fixed by someone else. That someone else was Lydia. I didn't meet her in those first two weeks. But I did feel her; in the moments before opening the door to that motel room, I would anticipate the clean room, the restored order, the lemon smell of wood polish, and in those days it was the only thing that gave me anything resembling relief.

Robert was in a coma for three days. He aspirated his own vomit when he was unconscious, and they think he was oxygen deprived for as long as three hours before the police discovered him in that barn. I sat by his bedside until he came out of it. I know it may sound perverse, but a part of me misses those hours with my son. My role, what I could do for him, had never been so clear. I had to be near him. I told him about his sisters and his mother, our dogs and the ugly house being built across the street in the woods where he used to play. I held his hand, which was something I'd never before done and have not done since. I wonder sometimes if it's like this with other fathers. What I know is that for me, having a son has been a difficult riddle, an awkward tiptoe between too tough and too easy. I never got the hang of it. Not like with my daughters, who were uncomplicated to be around, to love. The rules of engagement were much more obvious. Robert never liked sports. I think sometimes it was because when he was very young I was too busy with work and Kay and the girls to put a basketball in his hands and get him on the court. He liked his elaborate fantasy world of Dungeons & Dragons and the books he made, and he liked Tim, but he didn't have any interest in anything I knew about. When Kay was alive, she'd tell me it wasn't his job to be interested in me, it was my job to be interested in him. If she was right, and I expect she was, I failed at the job miserably. By the time he left for Harkness I had convinced myself that Robert was better off without my meddling, that he was self-sufficient and would navigate the world of boarding school and college just fine without knowing how to play basketball or a father who knew his way around the castles in Dungeons & Dragons. I can see now how self-serving that was.

After he came out of the coma, Robert remained in the ICU for nine days. He was conscious but vacant, and his speech was impaired. I sat with him like those first three days but I did not hold his hand. Of all the things to remember, it's hesitating with my hand that morning when he was newly awake and frightened, stumbling with the simplest words. That is a moment I would do differently if I had the chance. There are many. What could I have possibly been worried about? *Everything* is the answer. I was worried about everything. It's painful to admit, but when I remember that time, I see myself as a skittish fool, wringing my hands over every little decision and getting most of them wrong. Why is it only later that things begin to make sense? Mostly, I've made my peace with the mistakes I've made, but every so often I bump into a memory and it will sit me right down. Not swarming my boy with attention and love in those early years, not grabbing his hand and pulling him toward me as much as I could have, letting him disappear to boarding school because it felt at the time like one less thing to worry about. These are the regrets that slip and drop down, and when they do, there is nothing to be done, no action I can take to make it better. I just let them come for as long as they will.

After his time in the ICU, Robert was moved to the hospital's Acute Rehab Unit to try to get him walking, talking, and problem solving again. There was brain damage, but with work the doctors assured me it was likely he'd be fully functional, both physically and cognitively. They worked with him for nearly a month, and in that time I flew home for a night or two but for the most part stayed at the motel and saw Robert for breakfast and at the end of each day for dinner. The doctors wanted him to focus on the various therapies during the day, so I stayed away, worked from the motel room and spoke with Kay and my mother and sister, who were driving her to chemo and helping with the girls. Kay would ask about Robert but deflected any questions I asked about how she was feeling. She tried to be cheerful, but I could hear her fading away a bit more every time we spoke.

I met Lydia the day Robert was moved to the rehab unit and his doctor asked that I come back at the end of the day. For the first time since I'd checked in, I'd returned to the motel before nightfall. I could hear the vacuum cleaner going as I put the key in the door, and for a second I hesitated before opening. I wasn't sure I actually wanted to see who performed the daily magic of tidying the room and arranging my things so carefully. I enjoyed and imagined into the mystery, so before I turned the key in the lock, I stopped and listened to the hum of the vacuum, the sound of its being pushed along the floor and bumping gently into furniture. I must not have noticed it turn off because without warning the door opened, and suddenly there she was. In jeans and clinging white T-shirt, a pile of brown hair knotted loosely on her head, at least ten years younger than I was. Young. Beautiful. Lydia.

She rushed off that first day, and neither of us said more than awkward hellos. I came back the following morning after an early breakfast with Robert and she had not yet arrived. For some reason, I felt nervous. I began cleaning up the room and folding my clothes, which is what I ought to have done from the beginning. Her job was to clean the rooms, not pick up after the guests. I stopped short of making the bed and instead made sure the toilet was flushed, and I tidied a pile of hospital paperwork scattered on the desk. She turned up before noon and didn't bother with knocking. I suppose it hadn't occurred to her I'd be there, so she just used her key and came right on in. I was sitting in the chair by the bed and remained silent as she set her large plastic bucket with cleaning supplies down on the carpet inside the door. She was wearing the same jeans as the day before and again a T-shirt, but this time light blue instead of white. I said good morning and she screamed.

What happened over the next three weeks is not something I'm proud of, but it is not a regret. Not like so much else is. Lydia Morey was a sad young woman trapped in a bad marriage, and I was a frightened man who knew his wife would soon be dead. There was more—she was sexy. Young, healthy, and underneath those tight jeans and T-shirts, she had the curvy figure of a pinup. And though she was troubled, she was also tough in ways that let me know she'd be okay. That she'd figure her life out somehow and survive. I hope she did.

Mostly, we just talked. She told me about the father she did not know, her mother's sharp tongue and how she bullied her to stay with her husband despite his teasing and his violence. She talked about wanting to run away. Driving to some town in the Middle West somewhere where no one knew her and where she could begin again. It was surprising and sad to see someone so young feel so hopeless. I listened but I offered no solutions, no advice. How could I? My life was in tatters and I hadn't a clue what to do. She listened to me tell my tale of woe, and we were able to laugh at it all, even the over-dose, even the cancer. Our lives felt unreal and far away while we were in that motel room. As if we were telling stories of other people's lives to each other, not our own. Maybe it's what we both needed then. I don't know. What I do know is that it didn't feel bad or wrong. I'd never been unfaithful to Kay in the eighteen years of our marriage. Never been seriously tempted, either. But before I left the Betsy, two days before I returned to Atlanta, I went to bed with Lydia. It started when she kissed me. First on my forehead and then on my lips. We had been sitting on the bed and there had been a long silence. I had just told her I was taking Robert back to Atlanta to a hospital where he could continue his therapy. There was nothing to say. We both knew I would never come back to Wells, Connecticut, and to the Betsy. Our days together were about to be over. So she kissed me. And I kissed her back.

To this day I remember those hours with Lydia Morey as some of the sweetest and most desperate of my life. I wonder if she remembers them at all.

June

There are barely any clothes in Lolly's bag: one bathing suit, one sundress, panties, flip-flops, flats, two T-shirts, and a pair of men's pajamas stolen from Adam years ago. There are more vitamin bottles and notebooks than garments.

The man who reintroduced himself as Brody had walked her back to the car and drove her to a Super 8 motel less than a mile down the road. When she said she had no ID, he checked her in with his credit card and driver's license. He carried Lolly's duffel bag into the room, scribbled his number down, and told June he'd take the Subaru to his friend's garage nearby to put on a real tire and check the rest. He'd return it in the morning.

Right away, she collapsed. Curled under the sheets, the first she'd felt for more than a week, and slept until morning. She was awake when Brody came by to give her the car keys. She'd already been to the ATM in the lobby to get him money for the tire and the motel room. It was only two hundred dollars, the maximum she could withdraw. When he pushed it away, she folded the bills and slipped them into his jeans pocket. *You got more than you expected when I asked you for help,* she said, more words than she'd spoken in weeks.

I'm glad I was the one you asked, he replied, the first wrinkle of flirtation in his voice.

Once he has gone, she sits on the bed next to Lolly's duffel, which she has filled again, but not before folding and arranging each item carefully. She keeps the notebooks on the bed and sits next to them before pulling one to her lap. There are three, each with the same orange cover Lolly preferred since high school. And just as they had been then, the notebooks are bursting with folded papers, poems ripped from the pages of the *New Yorker*, illegible memos from the photo editor she'd been assisting at the fashion magazine where she'd started as an intern, crushed receipts, a MetroCard, take-out menus from the city, bills, pages torn from gallery catalogs. Lolly had always used these beat-up old notebooks as a kind of portable file cabinet for her life, but there was no order, no system. The one June holds was nearest the top of the duffel, beneath the light blue towel exploding with vitamin bottles. The cover is unmarked. She opens it, lightly brushes the pages with her fingertips. She remembers cataloging unfinished canvases by a painter she once represented who committed suicide. His family asked her to go through his apartment and studio and organize whatever she felt was important. She remembers finding an old Boy Scout manual filled with precise pencil drawings of animals—bears mostly, some gentle koalas and black-bear cubs, others angry, with teeth exposed and claws out. Very likely no one had ever seen these drawings, and she remembers having the fleeting instinct to steal the book and keep it herself. Something about it was so private and beautiful, so hopeful, even given the situation that would cause her to find it. She did not steal it but instead included it in a show at the gallery in New York and sold it to one of the artist's longtime collectors. It was one of the last shows she'd organized in New York before leaving for London.

On the first three pages of Lolly's notebook are floor plans of imaginary houses, each with one bedroom, several large public spaces, and two rooms labeled LOLLY'S STUDIO and WILL'S STUDY. Studio for what? June wonders. Lolly had dabbled in pastel drawings and watercolor painting early in high school, but June hadn't heard her mention any of that since. The pages that follow are filled with half-written poems, incomplete to-do lists, seating plans for the wedding reception. There are pages of sample menus from Feast of Reason that Lolly kept asking Rick to revise and reimagine. There are pictures of wedding cakes and flowers pulled from magazines; and there are late-bill notices from Con Ed for Lolly and Will's apartment in the city.

Lolly's electric bill, the unpaid caterer. This is the first time these neglected responsibilities have occurred to June. A bolt of panic, a feeling of having to take care of things, returns. It is an old, familiar feeling from another life. The one phone call she'd made was to Paul, her lawyer in the city, asking what she needed to do to give him power of attorney over everything—the insurance claims, the bank accounts, outstanding bills. She asked him to consolidate her bank accounts, liquidate her 401(k), pay whatever penalties needed to be paid, sell the property where the house had been, if it could be sold, and transfer any monies she had to her checking account so that she could access it through her debit card. Paul drove to Connecticut with the papers to be signed and brought someone from his office to notarize them. June told him on the phone that she did not want a discussion or to be advised, just this one thing done, and he could take what she owed him from the account he now con-trolled. She hoped Rick and anyone else she owed money to had found their way to Paul by now. June begins to make a mental list of who these people might be. Rick, Lolly's landlord in the city, Edith Tobin, the town tax collector. The names buzz like bees. She closes the first notebook and pulls another from the duffel bag. This one has Lolly's name written across the front and under-neath it a date. It's a sloppy date from two years ago, *Summer 2012*, which would have been when Lolly returned from her semester in Mexico City;

when she brought Will to Boston to meet Adam and then, after, to meet June. The meeting was brief. Dinner in New York. This was before Lolly would agree to meet Luke, so June went to the city alone and drove back the same night. She barely remembers Will. Lolly brought many boyfriends around over the years, so there was no reason to expect this one would be any different. Also, she hadn't seen Lolly since Christmas. She'd asked both Adam and June not to visit her in Mexico City. To give her a break, she had explained, from being their daughter.

June flips through the notebook and sees line drawings of Will. Page after page of profiles, details, his nose, his eyes, his collarbone. They are amateurish, but what strikes her is how detailed they are, how attentive. Lolly was always a bit hyper and distractible, as the bulging contents of her notebooks attested, but she'd obviously been paying close attention to Will. The sustained gaze required to create these drawings is patient, tender, intimate, and June struggles not to look away. She feels a sting of jealousy as she looks at a study of Will's wavy, brown hair from behind. It is by far the most delicate and intricately drawn. June flips past the images of Will and finds a page covered in dark blue ink. At first it appears like a densely scribbled doodle—a nonsensical mural of shapes and lines. But when she turns the notebook on its side, it becomes clear that Lolly had been trying to create an image of the ocean. Crudely sketched seabirds fly at odd angles in the two-inch gap between the jagged horizon line and the edge of the page. And beneath the birds rise elaborately drawn waves, within which June can make out the shapes of faces, hands, city buildings, a car, a plane, eyes, trees, a door. The effect is mesmerizing and she begins to feel dizzy. June gently shuts the notebook and puts it on the bed, folded papers and clippings jutting from its edges. Here, she recognizes, is a new regret. What she saw in the images of Will and even more clearly in the waves was someone attempting to make sense of the world by re-creating it, refracting and complicating its pieces in order to make meaning. What she saw was that Lolly was something she never imagined her to be: an artist. Maybe not a great one—if great could even be designated with empirical accuracy —but someone with an artistic soul who needed to abstract what puzzled her to find the answers. And June missed it. It didn't matter that she'd spent her career identifying and nurturing this very instinct in her clients. It didn't matter that this was the one part of her life where she had not failed. Lolly was an artist finding her way, and June missed it completely. She didn't know which was worse, that she missed it or that Lolly never shared it with her.

The dizziness gets worse and June places both

hands on the bed and steadies herself. She sits very still, her eyes closed and both feet planted firmly on the floor. She waits for it to subside, which, after a few minutes, it does. Eventually, she forces herself to pull the last notebook from the duffel. When she opens this one, she sees nothing is sketched or written on its pages, nothing stuck inside. It is new, its spine uncracked, and its pages blank. She closes the notebook and sees, written on its cover in brown marker, *Greece*.

June puts the notebook on the bed next to the other two and lies down. Her limbs feel leaden, numb. Her mind dulls. She slept for more than twelve hours the night before but is suddenly, again, tired. Moving slowly, she pulls her knees to her chest and closes her eyes.

There is a loud knock on the door. She has no idea how much time has passed. She notices that while asleep she has pushed the notebooks off the bed, and much of the wrinkled and folded contents have slid out across the thinly carpeted floor. *Hello. Hello in there. Checkout was two hours ago.* She blinks her eyes to understand where she is. *Okay, okay,* she calls, not knowing to whom or why. She looks at her feet and sees one of the notebooks faceup, opened to a drawing she hadn't seen earlier. It's of a one-story beach motel, scribbled in blue ink, with a sign in front that spells THE MOONSTONE. In front, there is an awkwardly sketched office and a row of cars;

behind the building is scrawled a greatly exaggerated depiction of crashing surf, spraying sea and foam to the top of the page. June picks the notebook up from the floor, places it in her lap, and flips to the next page. Written in blue ink, dated July 7, 2012, is a letter. The first word is *Mom.*

Lydia

She's warm, feels her skin getting damp under her clothes, so midstride, without slowing, she takes off her fleece pullover and folds it across her left arm. She's walking quickly. The cool air against her neck feels good. She breathes in deeply and wipes the sweat from her forehead. She remembers the money and double-checks the pocket to make sure it hasn't fallen out. Seven hundred dollars and the change from the fifty she used to pay for her coffee at the coffee shop. She can't believe the amount, or that she drove to the Walmart in Torrington to get the cash card Winton asked for and then mailed it away. Thank God, she thinks, it came back to her. She has enough money to live on from Luke's insurance and selling his business, but only if she lives cheaply, as she does. She squeezes the wad of bills in her pocket and thinks with a pulse of relief, Winton said they'd refund the lottery tax and they did. She starts to let herself imagine the whole ridiculous scheme is real. It's not so much the money that excites her as the possibility that Winton is telling the truth, that he's the friend he's sold himself to be. But so much of what he says does not add up. Is the refunded tax money just a way to get her to trust him? Set her up for a bigger haul? Winton did mention a handling charge a few phone calls before but said not to worry about it now, that it would be nothing compared to her windfall. She runs through the dozens of inconsistencies in his stories. When she challenged him once on the name of his ex-girlfriend, which changed nearly every time he mentioned her, he said, *Oh, Miss Lydia, I am not supposed to be getting so personal with you. I color some of the details to keep some privacy and protect you if my bosses ever found out we got to know each other as well as we have.* This was only a few nights ago, when the money had not yet arrived and she was beginning to worry. *We must be on each other's side, my friend, for us to get through this maze. For you to get your money and for me to leave this job. Can we be on each other's side?* he asked, and she answered after a short silence, *We can.*

Maybe he is exactly who he says he is, Lydia thinks as she quickens her step. Maybe he's not the enemy. When has she ever been right about anyone? She was wrong about Earl and Rex, and most men in between. And she was wrong about June. She remembers how at first she was sure the woman did not mean her or her son well. She could not fathom what this pampered New Yorker with a blond ponytail and perfectly manicured nails could want from her. And she had no interest in understanding what she wanted from her son. She remembers telling her to go away, to leave both of them alone. She had judged her before knowing anything about her. Had she also judged Winton too harshly? Might he actually be on her side? After all, he'd spent nearly three months talking on the phone to her. His stories kept changing but he kept telling them, kept calling each morning and each night. He did not go away, she reminds herself as she passes Edith Tobin's flower shop, which is more than she can say for June.

It is dark now and someone is behind her. She's heard footfalls but she does not want to stop, does not want to turn around. She is only six or seven driveways away from her apartment building. Her forehead beads with sweat and she can feel her jeans sticking to her legs. She holds her fleece with both hands against her chest. Only five driveways now. She hears a shoe scrape the sidewalk and something—a stick, a pebble— knocks against her calf. Someone is right behind her. She stops, spins around, and before she sees who is there, explodes *GET AWAY FROM ME!* Standing less than a foot from her is a boy wearing a green, hooded sweatshirt. Up close, she is certain this is Kathleen Riley's son. Same green eyes. Same thin lips. He looks directly at and then beyond Lydia, just over her shoulder. He begins to say something, *I'm . . . um . . . I know you . . . ,* but stops and rushes past her down the sidewalk toward the end of Upper Main and out of sight.

Lydia's blood is racing and she struggles to control her breathing. She checks the money in her fleece pocket and is relieved to feel it still there. She hurries the short distance to her building and fumbles with the key. Her hands are shaking. As soon as she gets the door open and closes it behind her, there is immediately a loud slamming on the windowpane. *BAM BAM BAM.* The boy, she thinks, he's followed her home. She pushes the full weight of her body against the door as she scrambles to lock the dead bolt. *STOP! STOP THIS!* she screams, her hands slick with sweat, the adrenaline streaking through her body like lightning. *WHAT DO YOU WANT FROM ME?* Her knees have buckled at the door. She cannot stand. As in nightmares from her childhood she has lost the power to move. The slamming returns and she crawls awkwardly away from the door. But when she gets enough distance to look back, she sees it is not the boy. It is a woman with a baby strapped in front of her in some kind of cloth carrier. Lydia closes her eyes and breathes. She calls out to the woman to hold on a second and manages to stand and walk into the kitchen to towel the perspiration from her face. Once her breathing steadies and her heart calms, she unlocks the door. *I'm so sorry,* she explains, *I thought you were someone else.* But the woman is unmoved. She is young, with tanned skin, short dark hair, and deep lines around her mouth and eyes. Once the door fully opens she steps forward and with her free hand strikes Lydia, hard, across her right cheek. *THAT's for my father!* she yells. She pulls her arm back to strike again but hesitates and steps back outside the apartment door. She looks as nervous as she is angry. *Whoever you are, if you don't give me the money my father sent to you, I will call the police and have you arrested. And don't deny it. . . . I know who you are and I know from the address those monsters in Jamaica gave him that you're the one who he sent the money to. You people are destroying him. . . . He's an old, lonely man and it's disgusting that you'd prey on an easy target like him. He actually believes there are millions of dollars with his name on it somewhere! He actually believes you people are his champions!* Stunned, Lydia reaches into her pocket, her fingers shaking, her mind still processing what she's just heard. Whoever this woman's father is must have fallen for Winton's scam, too, she thinks, handing the woman the seven hundred-dollar bills along with the loose pile of twenties, fives, and ones. He must have believed, as she had, that he was paying the tax to advance closer to the big prize. And this woman, his daughter, has mistaken her to be part of the con and not just like him. An easy target, lonely, someone willing to believe lies and throw money away in order to not be alone. The woman leans in, snatches the money from Lydia's hand, and tucks it into the pockets of her white corduroy trousers. The baby, who has until now remained silent, begins to cry. Whether it is a boy or a girl, Lydia cannot tell, but the crying becomes screaming—urgent, high-pitched screaming, as if someone has pinched the infant's skin. Tiny hands, red and desperate, reach up from the swaddle of pale yellow cloth bundled against the woman's chest. *You need to stop what you are doing,* she says seriously, oblivious to the exploding child. She holds Lydia's gaze for one more beat and, as she pulls the door shut behind her, says seriously, *You need to stop.* The silence that follows is complete. There are no sounds in the apartment. No cars driving past or people hollering anywhere. Lydia stands next to the door, locks it, and leans against the wall. The phone rings and she lets it. It stops for a few minutes and then begins again and the pattern goes on for over an hour. Finally, she crosses the living room into the kitchen and waits. After a minute the phone rings again and she picks up. It is, of course, Winton. He speaks her name, once and then again, but she says nothing. She is not playing games or holding back. She has no words. The boy on the sidewalk, the slap, the screaming child. She has been shocked into silence. Winton speaks again. *Lydia, come back to Earth. Come back down here to Mother Earth.* She's heard these words before.

Who else said this to her? Rex. The last man she called a boyfriend. *Come back to Earth, space cadet,* he used to say. *Touch down, spacey.* Who else but Rex. She can still feel the sting from the woman's slap on her cheek and something her mother used to say to her bubbles up. *One of these days someone is going to knock some sense into you.* It is not a happy memory; her mother would only ever say it when she was angry or drunk, but something about it makes Lydia laugh. She pictures her mother at that kitchen table, wagging her finger, drinking her schnapps, barking her warnings. She cannot help but laugh.

Lydia? Are you somewhere there? Winton. She forgot for a moment he was on the other end of the line. *My dear Lydia,* he says, *my dear, what is wrong?* She hears his concerned tone, the extra careful wording, but it does not soothe her. He continues to say her name, asks what could possibly be the matter. That voice, she thinks, and laughs again. I have sent money in the mail to someone I do not know, and I have been attacked in my own home. For a voice. A stranger's voice.

Tell me what troubles you, the voice coos. *Tell me.* Again, she thinks of Rex. The last man who lied to her as much as Winton has, she thinks, the last man like him who had the power to make her do things she knew were wrong. Again, she is quiet. After a long silence, Winton says again and gently, *Tell me what's wrong.*

Do you really want to know? she asks, feeling, against her will, the desire to tell him about her crazy evening. She holds the receiver to her ear and recognizes that besides Winton there is no one she can tell—about the boy following her home, the furious woman slapping her face, anything. She leans forward and drops the receiver to her lap. The voice in her hands is all she has and it's nothing. She rocks gently and wishes she could vanish. She feels more alone now than in the weeks after Luke's death. After a while, she hears Winton's voice coming from the phone. She puts the receiver to her ear and hears him chanting to himself, almost singing. *Oh, Miss Lydia, where have you gone? What have you done and where are you? Come back to me, miss.*

I'm here, she whispers. *I never went anywhere. I'm right where I've always been.*

Winton's voice falls to a whisper. *Tell me a story, my dear Lydia. Take a load off your soul. Tell me the truth because it will set you free.*

Lydia hears the creak of footsteps in the apartment above her. She listens to her upstairs neighbor walk across his kitchen, open the refrigerator door, and shut it softly. She hears the pop of a beer bottle opening and the clack of the tossed cap in the sink. She sits up straight, her back against the wooden chair. When she speaks, her voice scratches in her throat. *I'll tell you a story, Winton. The one about where I've always been.*

Lolly

Mom,

I'm writing to you from the edge of the world. It truly feels like we are in some place between earth and heaven here on the beach in Moclips. We checked in two nights ago after driving for four straight days from New York. Can you believe we got pulled over in New Jersey on Route 3? Right out of the gate, bam, a $125 speeding ticket. I'm sure the cop saw Will's Washington State plates and said, Let's get him. Anyway, we thought it was a bad omen for our trip, but instead it turned out that every moment after has been charmed, like we've had a lucky star guiding us the whole way. Even when we got lost in Pennsylvania it led us to stay in the most beautiful little town that's almost exclusively Amish. They couldn't have been nicer. We'd heard about a group of teenagers who flipped their car—Amish kids getting drunk and living it up in their purgatory year between high school and marriage. The whole town seemed to be shaped around those dead kids. Like if you looked closely you could see each one in the places where they once were. It's strange to say but I feel like I know them, a little. There was so much talk of them. That town was so sad but it was also beautiful to see a community need each other so much. And their faith. I have never believed in God though I can see how believing in one would help in the aftermath of the kind of tragedy they'd been through.

You can't imagine how many stars fill the sky here. They are brighter than the moon. Or the sound of the wind and the crashing waves. Like freight trains outside the window. It's not frightening, because for some reason this simple room at the edge of the world feels like the safest place I've ever been.

I know I'm rambling, Mom, but I'm in a mood, as Dad would say. Crossing this country, ending up here where Will grew up—I now understand why it was so important to him to show me—and the crazy wind has me thinking. It's funny to think that the wind has a shape but it does. It becomes visible every once in a while— in rain being driven to the ground in sheets, or in the snow on the fields behind our house. I remember looking out the window of my room in the winter, watching the wind blow on the surface of the white fields, lifting and whipping the snow into spirals, and in a flash you could see this force that was always there come to life and reveal itself. I think it is this way with children and parents. They are always there and then suddenly through some shock or disappointment or great gesture or absence the child sees this person who was there all the while— invisible to them beyond their function to provide. This is how it's been for me, with you. I only really saw you once you left Daddy, and I didn't like what I saw. I couldn't understand why you would leave him after all those years together. How you could choose your career over both of us. I still don't understand if I'm really being honest. But it's only lately that I can see that what I can and can't see doesn't matter. I don't have the right to say who you are with or not and it is not my right to know. With Luke in your life now, you have really snapped into view as a woman, like me, with the full menu of wants and desires as the rest of us. I'm not saying this has been much fun or not embarrassing; I'm ashamed to say it's both. But it has shaken things up. I'm sorry I refused to meet him in New York. I didn't want him to overshadow Will. And if I'm honest about it, I think I was worried how I would react and I didn't want Will to see me out of control.

Speaking of control, I guess Dad has come into view more, too. I've known for a long time about his desperate womanizing. It's always made me sad, but it's something I never held him accountable for. I blamed it on you, as I have many things. It never occurred to me until recently that maybe his childish way with women preceded your leaving and that it most likely had a lot to do with it. I can't believe this never really occurred to me before. I also can't claim to have come to some of these ideas on my own. Early on with Will he told me that it would be a good idea to question everything I thought I knew about Dad, you, your marriage, my childhood, myself even. Actually, he suggested that whenever I was resistant to a differing opinion about anything, I should try this out. Here I think he was talking about politics, him being much more sympathetic to our president than I am. Still, it's been difficult to pull back the curtain on old stories and old opinions. I've been doing it for a while now and it's humbling to see things more as they were and less as I have felt them to be over the years. What I'm trying to say is that I've been punishing you for a long time for not making the choices I wanted you to make, and as Will snores next to me now and before the sun comes up in a few hours I just want you to know that I see things a little more clearly now and I hope you can forgive me for being unable to sooner. I still get furious when I think of how you left and the way you made all these decisions without including me. You just announced the new order of things as if none of it had anything to do with me. Can you possibly imagine how that felt at fourteen? Or how lonely it was after you left? Did you even think about me when you made all these decisions? Did you ever think how much I would miss you?

Here I go. It takes so little to go back to all that. But I suppose that's why I'm writing to you now. To be completely honest, it's something Will suggested I do. To write to you without worrying about you reading the words. To just say what I feel without risking being held to any of it. He told me to do this months ago but every time I tried I couldn't. But tonight feels different. Something about this place.

And Will. I want with you what he has with his parents. It's so uncomplicated with him! He just loves them and it's so easy and affectionate between them. I want that but I don't know how to get it. It's like if I just let you off the hook for everything, I've betrayed myself. Or the self I was. And that's when I get stuck. But as Will and I move ahead together, I'm feeling like it's getting easier to let go of some of the stuff I've been hanging on to.

What I want to say is that I don't want to go back to or stay stuck in the way things have been between us. Everything seems so delicate and brief and I don't want us to be so apart anymore. I don't know how to say any of this to you, which is why I am writing it down. I hope I give you this someday.

Love,
Lolly

Silas

He is pedaling as fast as he can out of town and toward home. He cannot shake the frightened look on her face, her voice yelling. He has imagined them meeting many times but never once the way it went tonight. When he's pictured it, she is warm, comforting, tucking him into her large bosom and stroking his head. He has imagined her without her clothes, kissing his chest, holding his dick. He has imagined her cutting his dick off, too, to punish him, and throwing it in Indian Pond. He has imagined Lydia Morey every which way, but never how he saw her tonight. She was terrified, and maybe in one of his fantasies it would have turned him on, but this time it did just the opposite. It rattled him. Exposed her beyond the limited versions of her he'd been working with. This was not lonely or angry or lusty or grieving. This was human. And it's much more than he can handle.

He turns off Tate Lane down a dirt road. Once he's out of sight of passing cars, he jumps off the bike and let's it crash to the ground. He unhooks the knapsack from his shoulders, the yellow canvas hardly visible. He cannot see his hands or fingers clearly, but he knows the surfaces and shapes of his stuff: Tupperware container, bowl, water bottle, bong, and lighter. He sloppily packs an untidy hit and lights it. He smokes it down and quickly packs and lights a second. The pot is a mix of some old stuff from Charlie and a few new buds he stole from a neighbor who hides his plants in plain sight along the back row of his vegetable garden. It's a strong blend, and soon he feels a thick film rise between this moment and the last few hours. He regards it all now, dimly, as through a foggy snow globe, and for that he is grateful. He leans against a tree and sees Lydia's face again. He can now slow the incident down and watch her eyebrows rise, her mouth widen as she yells at him. She's covering her chest with her coat, but now that he's in charge of the scene, he has her drop it and he looks down her low-scooped T-shirt as she bends to pick it up. Now the T-shirt is sweaty and soaked, and through the translucent cloth he sees pink skin, dark, wide nipples. The vision relaxes him, helps him shake off the feelings from before. He packs up his gear, zips the knapsack, and throws it over his shoulder. He walks his bike back to Tate Lane. Above him, the moon is nearly full and glows pink in the chilly night. Thin clouds inch slowly across the sky, and on the surface of the moon he begins to make out a face. At first it is a rough mask with uneven eyebrows and lopsided whiskers, the mouth and nose disfigured and huge. Then it comes alive. He knows this face.

It's the dragon he saw last May on his way home from June Reid's house. Back then, his ruby wings and infinite tail filled the sky, but now they are invisible, cloaked in the blue-black night. Only the snout, the devil eyes, and the smoke pouring from its throat are visible. It's him. He knows he is hallucinating, but still, his hands shake as he pulls his bike toward him. As he gets on, he hears something. A voice, a growl, a barking dog. He cannot tell. But in that noise he hears *GO* as clear and precise as anything he has ever heard. He begins to pedal and looks up at the moon. The dragon's face is fully articulated: snout high, mouth wide. The eyes do not shift their gaze from him. He looks behind the moon and begins to see the outline of its mammoth body, the silhouette of its batlike wings etching the sky. He is in the middle of the road, pedaling slowly and looking up and behind him at the same time. When he starts to trace the ridges on its epic tail, the handlebars twist in his hands, the front tire jerks to the left, and the bike collapses onto the pavement. As he falls, landing on his side, he hears a crack underneath him, the loose arrangement of bong and Tupperware breaking his fall, and then the bong, he can feel as well as hear, breaking to bits. He sits in the road, checks his limbs to see that everything still works. He feels along his side and shoulders to make sure none of the glass has speared him. He can detect no serious injuries, but he's scraped the skin off his palms, and the exposed flesh begins to sting. Sitting in the middle of the road, he dares to look up, and sure enough the dragon is beaming, amused, directly at him. *What the fuck? What!* he calls out, half crying from frustration and fear. *GO? Go where? WHERE AM I SUPPOSED TO GO?*

He is demanding answers from the enchanted arrangement of cloud and night and moon, but he knows where he has to go. He has not been back there since May when he ran across the lawn and up the driveway to the road. *Fuck,* he mumbles, pulling the bike from the road and wiping the loose asphalt from the cuts on his hands. He rides in the direction of home but passes Wildey Road, where he lives, and continues on Indian Pond. He refuses to look up at the night sky until he gets there, and as he passes the pond, he can see the pattern of blues and grays and blacks reflecting in the water. He cannot help but look, and the kaleidoscopic pattern shimmering there is both ominous and beautiful. Oncoming lights from up the road break the spell and he slows his bike until the car passes. By the time it does, he is beyond the church, and soon he is at the top of the driveway.

June

She knows now where this will end. Where the land runs out and there is only sea, and between the two, a room. The pages of the letter are tucked into the orange notebook that sits on top of the other two in the passenger seat next to her. At the Super 8, she read each word, again and then again, until the manager demanded she leave immediately or pay for another night. The handwriting was familiar, undeniably Lolly's, but the words were not. They were from someone she only dimly remembered, from before she and Adam told Lolly they were divorcing. After that, Lolly was never as candid or open or as affectionate with June. She could see in the letter Lolly's conflicted attempt to describe a future she had yet to occupy. She never got there, June thinks, remembering the cold exchange with Luke on the porch the night before the wedding. But she was trying. Wherever she'd been by the time she died, it was much closer than June knew. To be given a glimpse now was a bitter miracle, a ghostly caress that left more regret than solace.

As she crosses out of Idaho into Washington State, she breathes in Lolly's scent. She'd sniffed it earlier, wafting off the pages, faintly, the strange perfume that smelled like hot chocolate that

Will gave her during their semester in Mexico and continued to supply her with after. June rummaged through Lolly's bag and found the small, brown-and-white bottle and sprayed her wrists, lightly, and the pages, before folding them into the notebook and leaving the Super 8. The smell of cocoa and cinnamon fills the car. How could she have allowed so much distance between them?

She hears Luke's voice, yelling, as if in answer, *Jesus, June, throw it!* He is running away from her in the lawn behind the house. *Throw it! Throw it!* He is shouting to her as she kneads the hard plastic rim of the Frisbee in her hands. *What are you afraid of?* He calls, standing still now, arms crossed against his chest. It was the second summer, the one after he moved in, and he'd insisted they go outside and toss the Frisbee. They'd made it as far as the lawn, but something in her refused to throw it. She can't remember what it was—the childishness of the game? That he had asked for something, demanded it, and she had the power to refuse? After a while he walked off, chilly and disappointed. There were moments like this when she could not be what he wanted and yet he would insist. It was like a game of chicken and she always won. She never blinked, and as with the Frisbee, he usually stormed off in a huff. Just like Lolly had so many times. She remembers how that yellow Frisbee sat in the lawn for weeks, neither of them willing to retrieve it. Luke even mowed around the thing and let a little thicket of grass grow up in a rough circle where it lay. He never mentioned it; nor did she. And then one day it was gone.

Her right hand strays from the steering wheel and rests on the notebook next to her. Her fingers brush the worn surface of the cover and then she pulls it to her lap, where she lets it rest. She breathes in Lolly's scent and relaxes her foot from the gas pedal. She is careful to maintain precisely the speed limit, as she does not want anything to stop her from getting to the Moonstone. If she stops for gas only, she will be there before evening. There is no reason to rush other than the feeling she's had since reading the letter: that she needs to see the inside of that room, hear the wind howl and the waves crash as Lolly described, see the same stars and moon, breathe the same salt air. It is not her daughter she is driving to, but it is as close as she will ever get.

She is hours away. She will drive until the road runs out, and she will find that room, and she will stay.

Dale

Our plan had been to wait a year before heading up from Portland to Moclips with Will's ashes, but after the first gentle day in February, when the cold rains slowed and the relief of spring was, if not actually near, imaginable, Mimi said it was time. I called the Moonstone and asked if Room 6 was free the following weekend, and the woman who answered said it was not and that likely it wouldn't be for a long while. Someone had checked in at the beginning of July and never left. I thought it was strange, since the Moonstone is hardly the kind of place you imagine someone calling home, but I was disappointed, too, as Room 6 meant something to Will. It was where he proposed to Lolly, and where he stayed when he returned to attend Joseph Chenois's memorial. It would have been nice to stay in Room 6, see what Will saw during those trips back to Moclips, but it wasn't the reason we were going.

Will never told us where he wanted to be buried or have his ashes scattered—why would he at twenty-three years old? but we knew. A stretch of beach, no longer than a mile, runs between the Moonstone and the Quinault reservation, the ocean on one side and the small, gray house where he grew up, with us, on the other. There was no place he loved more. No place he felt as safe. It was his home and it gave us some comfort to think of him there. So for the first time since we'd lived there together as a family, we returned to Moclips.

When we arrived at the Moonstone, the dusty black wagon parked by the Dumpster looked like it hadn't been driven in years. The blue license plate below the back hatch was hardly visible, but we knew right away it was from Connecticut and we knew it was June's. My first instinct was to stop the car, put it in reverse, and drive away. I felt like we had stumbled upon something too personal to barge in on. I assumed, since this was where Will and Lolly got engaged, she had come to be close to her daughter, just as we had come to be close to our son. Unsure what to do, we parked the car next to the office and sat silently for a long time. Eventually, Mike and Pru said we were being ridiculous and that maybe it wasn't even June's wagon. So we went into the office, met the new owners, and got keys to two rooms. Rooms 5 and 7, the only two left and of course on either side of Room 6. None of us mentioned to Rebecca and Kelly that we knew June. Not even when Kelly apologized again about Room 6 not being available. We didn't decide on this in the car or even signal nonverbally to each other in the office; it was just something we all understood. If she was there, we'd leave her alone as best we could, though given the steps she'd taken to avoid us and everyone else it was hard to imagine she'd stay once she knew we'd arrived.

I don't know why or how, but through all these months of June's not returning our phone calls or responding to the letters we mailed to her, care of her lawyer in New York, I knew she was okay. Mimi had wondered if we shouldn't make a greater effort to locate her: call the artists she'd represented, interrogate the lawyer, track down relatives, though there was never any mention of uncles or aunts or cousins. A few weeks after Christmas, I called information and asked for Lydia Morey's phone number and got it right away. I didn't know who else to call, and at first, maybe because of the speculation that her son, Luke, may have had something to do with the accident, I'd put it off. But she was the only person from that town we knew who might know where June was. Besides Luke, June was not a terribly connected person. She had no friends who we knew to be close to her. She had left her job at a gallery in London years before, and whatever work life she had was, to us, invisible. By the number of people who'd turned up at the church that morning and by the pictures on June's bookshelves and walls, it appeared she had lived a full and peopled life, but it didn't seem like anyone, besides Luke, had stuck. Including, unfortunately, her daughter, who, according to

209

Will and from what we could see ourselves, mostly stayed away. Given this, it's maybe not so surprising that Lolly clung to our family. Will often joked that she settled on him only so she could get to us. And it's true, I did notice how she would sometimes watch Will with Mimi or with Pru and Mike. She would watch them like her nose was pressed to the glass wall of an aquarium, watching exotic fish move in water, or how a scientist would observe rare bats in the wild. She said to us when we first met her in Mexico City that her parents didn't know how to do it, and when we asked her what, she said, *Everything*. It was sad to hear a child speak so frankly and judgmentally about her parents, and for a while Mimi worried that Lolly was too cynical, too tough-minded and negative for Will. I worried, too, but Will was clearly in love, and I knew that nothing could be done if someone felt that way about another person, especially your child. Lolly was different, certainly on the self-centered and selfish side, but she was at her core kind and she adored Will and we could do nothing, so we embraced her. I think Will sensed that despite her girlish manner, something was broken in her. Mimi says wounds can sing a beguiling song, and for Will—who from boyhood felt compelled to fix and help and take care of nearly everything and anyone in his path—Lolly's song was irresistible.

Outside the subject of her family, Lolly was

lighter and more open, so we tended not to bring them up, so when we finally met Adam, and later, June and Luke, we knew little about any of them. Mimi and I had pieced together that relations were difficult between June and Adam. He had various girlfriends whom Lolly didn't respect; and once June began her relationship with Luke, Lolly at first refused to acknowledge him and for the most part avoided her mother. She talked to Pru about it the week before the wedding and, of course, Will, but I don't really know what went on between Lolly and her mother. Clearly they had much to resolve, and according to Pru, among the many sad things about what happened is that they had, in those months leading up to the wedding, just begun.

When I spoke to Lydia in January, she told me June had been gone since early summer and that she had not seen or heard from her since the funeral. She said that what remained of the house had been demolished, and a chain now blocked the driveway from the road. She reported the news dispassionately, as if she had little to do with any of it, or with June, which surprised me, since the two of them, from what I could see in those few days before the wedding, seemed close. At the rehearsal, June fixed Lydia's hair and both of them laughed secretively, like old friends. I can still picture them, side by side, talking in the church, on the lawn, at the sink, on the porch. I remember them more with each other than apart. They were a funny pair, very different in superficial ways—one sleek and blond, the other earthy, with long, dark hair falling down everywhere; one poised and stoic, the other needier, less sure. Still, they were much the same in how they approached their children: formal and timid, careful, as if they had only just met them. But with each other they appeared relaxed, natural. So to hear Lydia talk about June with such distance was a surprise, but then I remembered June at the funeral and the days before. She didn't speak. Not to us, not to Lydia, not to anyone. I remember how she pivoted away from each of us when addressed, and if hugged, she held still, hands at her sides, until it was over. We reached out to her as best we could, but we were in shock, and instinctively we closed ranks among ourselves. We were out of our minds and away from home. Our boy was gone.

There had been rumors right away about Luke causing the explosion. The day we left Wells, the woman at the front desk at the Betsy told us she always knew something terrible was going to happen the moment she heard Lydia Hannafin's boy moved into June Reid's house. *Bound to end badly,* she said, shaking her head and sounding perversely satisfied. The four of us stayed quiet and left the small lobby as quickly as possible.

We chose to believe that what happened was a

horrible accident, nothing more and nothing less. Anyone who had ever been in that kitchen knows it had to have been something to do with the stove. It looked like something from the Depression era. Rusty and white, tilting at an angle. I remember the afternoon before the rehearsal watching June fussing over one of the burners to boil water for tea, muttering when it wouldn't light right away. If I blame anyone, it's June. She should have taken care to replace that treacherous appliance. It was so clearly not safe. She had the means, and the rest of the property was well maintained, meticulous even. I try not to think about it, but at times I catch myself wondering how on earth could she have missed this one thing. How could she have been so careless? Knowing that June must agonize over these same questions dulls with pity, but does not eradicate, the anger I can still feel.

What was left of that old stove, the house, and any clues to what exactly caused the explosion were destroyed the day after the accident, bulldozed and dragged away by the state, though no one knew why. Our family is certain that Luke did not set out to hurt anyone. He was a decent man, and despite tensions in the house that night and even the days before, he was no killer. If it was due to some carelessness on his part, the boy paid a high price and God bless his tortured soul. His time in jail and his being black made him an easy scapegoat in that town, which you could hardly call racially diverse. Will, who planned on becoming a public defender in communities that didn't have adequate representation, would have been livid to see how swiftly the finger was pointed. So with so much unknown, our family chose to follow Will's lead and let go of any theories or blame. This doesn't mean we haven't suffered, we have. And it doesn't mean we've found peace.

After we returned to Portland, there was a period when Mike wouldn't speak to us because we hadn't pressed for more of an investigation right after the accident. He insisted we hire a lawyer to sue the fire department, or the town, I can't remember now exactly who he had in his crosshairs. Maybe we should have. But when I question our choice to walk away, I realize that whatever punishment we might have unleashed on the clumsy small-town officials responsible for destroying our chance for answers, or even if through some great show of force or determination or luck we actually found out what happened that night, there would be no changing the awful truth: Will is gone. We will never again see or hear or be with our magical son.

Mike has come around, but it's still not easy. We see him less, but Mimi and I know it's just for now. Pru has taken time away from graduate school and moved back home. Her friends from

Moclips and college call and occasionally drop by, but she keeps to herself, reads novels she's read before at the kitchen table until after midnight and sleeps in late. For now, we just give her space and let her be. And Mimi and I still teach—her third grade and me fifth—and we do what we've done for years: encourage and discipline, scribble what needs to be learned on chalkboards, and keep watch as the young people who come under our care for a short while hurry by on their way to the world.

We talk less now. There are car rides and Sunday mornings and entire meals when Mimi and I don't speak a word to each other. Not out of anger or punishment, but we've learned that grief can sometimes get loud, and when it does, we try not to speak over it.

I'm ashamed to remember that we did not reach out to Lydia sooner than we did. Good reason or not, we kept our distance from her in those unreal days between what happened and the funerals. She lost her son the same way we had, and still we had no words for her. When we spoke in January, I told her I was sorry it had been so long since she'd heard from us, and that she had been and would continue to be in our prayers. I asked her to let us know if June turned up, and she said of course and I promised the same. We stayed on the line for a few breaths of uncomfortable silence, and then we said good-bye.

A month later, from the Moonstone, Mimi dialed Lydia's number again, but it just rang and rang. We tried a few more times but each time it was the same. This was the day after we checked in, when we first saw June. It was early, and Mimi and I had been up and showered and getting ready to go for a walk down the beach and around the old neighborhood. Just before we left the room, we saw June cross like a ghost in front of our window. She was wearing the same clothes she wore the night of the rehearsal and the unreal days after. It was just a moment, but she looked the same, only thinner, less animated. We didn't see her again until that evening, just after the sun had gone down. The four of us had walked to the water's edge at sunset to spread Will's ashes. The surf was rough and the cloud cover was thick, so there was no grand ceremonial sunset as we'd hoped. Just the chilly surf and a pewter sky and Pru, knee-deep in the ocean, shaking the small ceramic container where we'd kept Will's ashes all year. Once the last bit of ash had finally disappeared, Pru came back to where we stood on the beach. We circled her and, with Mike, threw our arms around each other and we wept. We stood together for a long time. I've never been one to go to church, but I've always believed in a creative intelligence behind the ongoing riddle of the world. To that great force I prayed to guide Will's soul wherever it was and to protect my family. The second prayer was a selfish one. Shoulder to shoulder on that beach I couldn't bear the idea of losing any of them. Yet I knew we would, one by one, lose each other. Life never felt so gifted. Mike let go first and nudged us away from the encroaching water. Reluctantly, I let go, too, and we began to make our way back to our rooms.

A light mist was in the gusting wind, and by the time we reached the Moonstone we were drenched. The lights in Room 6 were on, and as we neared the building, we saw Cissy step out the door, shut it behind her, and head toward home. Before the door was closed all the way, we could see June, arms across her chest, standing very still. She did not see us, nor did Cissy. How strange it was to see such a significant figure from Will's past, from ours, leaving June Reid's room. And how strange that Cissy hadn't come by to see us since Rebecca and Kelly must have told her we'd checked in. Whatever her reasons, when Mimi and I got back to the room that night, we tried Lydia's number one more time, only to hear it ring without answer. Mimi pulled a pen from her purse and began writing a note on the small pad of Moonstone stationery. We'd get an envelope and stamp from Kelly the next morning and post it to Lydia with an address no more specific than Main Street, Wells, Connecticut. We hoped it would find her.

Lydia

The kitchen is dark. A tinny laugh track from the TV in the apartment upstairs spells the silence. Lydia pulls her chair closer to the kitchen table, and as she does, it softly scrapes the floor. She holds the receiver to her ear with both hands and asks Winton if he is still there.

Always, he answers calmly, as if he's been waiting to say this exact word.

Good . . . just stay there. Lydia draws in a deep breath and exhales slowly. She's still shaking from her run-in on the sidewalk with the boy who must be Kathleen Riley's son and the woman who slapped her minutes ago, but she's not afraid. She closes her eyes as she speaks.

I never told you about Rex. He's someone I met at the Tap a long time ago. The Tap is a bar that's been here forever and will stay here forever like the people who drink there. People like me. And like Earl, who went there every night until they threw him out for good a few years after we divorced. It takes a lot to get banned from the Tap, so that should give you an idea of the kind of guy he is. I guess if Earl hadn't been thrown out of the Tap, I'd never have started going there in the first place, so if you think about it, I have Earl to thank for Rex. This was a long time after Earl, but I was still young enough to go there and not pay for drinks.

Maybe this starts with the fact that I was in my forties and still expecting free drinks. You've never seen me, Winton, but until not too long ago I could turn a few heads. It never did me any good, but it got me free drinks and that night it got me Rex. Rex was not from here but not from too far either. He owned a gym in Amenia and had a bunch of small businesses. I never could keep track of what he was doing, and he always had a story to explain a new car or a new motorcycle. Things sort of fell into his lap—TVs, log splitters, tires, snowmobiles—and I never understood exactly how. It didn't matter to me. He was funny and liked to take me to nice restaurants. This was when I still thought going to a nice restaurant meant something.

Lydia's voice has risen. She is not shouting, but she speaks with purpose, and swiftly, with the energy that comes from making connections, detecting a pattern, figuring something out. It is, she knows soon after she begins, a story she's in a hurry to finish.

Besides my son and my ex-husband, Earl, the longest relationship I've had with a man is with Rex. Luke was in high school then and still living with me, but he was never around. He had swimming practice and college applications and whatever girlfriend he was running with.

When Rex came along, it felt good to have my own plans, different company besides my son, who'd been my whole life since he was born. It felt a little too good because I didn't pay close enough attention to what should have been warning signs. Rex would disappear for a few days without giving me a heads-up, and at first it seemed strange but after a while I got used to it. Also, there were stories that didn't add up—like yours, Winton, names that would change, places and times that didn't match—but I got used to that, too, and told myself none of it mattered. When he was around, Rex was fun. He could be mysterious and unreliable, but he made me laugh. Like Earl could. Like you.

Luke never bothered me about Rex. He was respectful, but I could tell he didn't like him. He never said so, but with Luke you could always tell how he felt about someone by the way he listened to them.

His face would either be open or closed—there is no better way to describe it—and with Rex he was closed, like he knew whatever was coming out of his mouth was bullshit. This was not a talent he got from me. I've only ever recognized bullshit once I was covered in it. Like now.

A few weeks after Luke graduated from high school, Rex asked to borrow the car. It was on a Saturday afternoon that he asked, and he needed it to run errands the next day. Something was wrong with his Corvette, he told me, and promised he'd have the car back by evening. I remember Luke was annoyed because our deal was that I had the car for work during the week and he could use it on weekends. I don't remember what I said exactly, but reluctantly he agreed.

So Rex slept over Saturday night, and on Sunday morning, before I was awake, he took off. Three or four hours later he called me from a jail in Beacon. He'd been pulled over by a state trooper near Kingston, and a large amount of cocaine was found in the car. He asked me to post bail but I didn't have access to that kind of money; so his lawyer, a man with a woman's name, Carol, somehow got the money and he was out the next morning. What Rex told me outside the courthouse that day was that the drugs were not his. That they were Luke's and that he'd been hiding them in the car. He even said he'd heard him on the phone arranging drop-offs and deals and never told me because he wanted to protect me. Winton, you told me you wanted to protect me, too. Do you remember? From your bosses? Why would I need you to protect me from people who run a lottery I'd supposedly won? That's when I should have hung up the phone on you, but I didn't. And when Rex told me he'd been protecting me from the truth about Luke, I should have turned my back and walked away. But I didn't. I listened. Just like I listened to you. I actually listened. I listened to his lawyer, too, who told me that Luke would be in jail for ten years if he didn't plead guilty. A few days later, I listened to the DA, who told me the drugs were in one of Luke's gym bags with his school ID and other belongings, some swim goggles and a portable CD player. He also told me that a dealer from White Plains, a guy by the name of Ray Hale, who'd been busted around the same time, gave a statement that Luke was his distributor in Litchfield County. He said he also had two more people to testify that they'd bought cocaine from Luke. When I found out that Rex and this Ray Hale had the same lawyer, Rex told me it was a coincidence, that there are only so many people who handle drug cases in the Hudson Valley. And guess what? I believed him. I believed all of them. All of them except my son, who begged me to get him a good lawyer, who recruited teachers and coaches and friends to testify and write letters on his behalf. Everyone in his life stood by him, but I failed him. I did worse than fail him.

The afternoon after Rex's arrest, three police officers showed up at the apartment with a search warrant. I called Luke's public defender, who said they had probable cause because not only did they have depositions claiming Luke was a dealer, they found the drugs in his gym bag in a car that he drove regularly. He told me I didn't have a choice but to let them search the place. So I let them in, and as if they'd been given a map in advance they went straight to Luke's bedroom and in less than a few minutes found two more bags of cocaine stuffed in a coffee can under his bed. It was like being in a nightmare. Luke, who had been watching from the hallway with me, went crazy. Yelling that he'd been framed, that Rex must have planted the drugs there in case he was caught. He yelled at me, too. Told me I had ruined his life by bringing Rex into our lives. I don't think I really understood how right he was until the police officers wrestled him to the kitchen floor and handcuffed him while one of them read his rights. And still, I didn't protect him. I should have thrown myself on that car and screamed and yelled until the cops and the judges and the lawyers all believed that I was the one responsible for the drugs. I should have been the one to go to prison. My life was nothing and Luke's was just beginning. But I did not move. I did not yell. I did nothing as I watched the police drive my son away.

Lydia lowers the phone to her chest. Her face is a mix of agony and disbelief, and when she returns the receiver to her ear, her voice is softer than before, less hurried.

I know you think I'm a stupid woman, Winton, but even you won't believe the next part. The next part is possible only when you have a weak woman who is afraid to be alone. Whose son has a scholarship to a school on the other side of the country and is leaving without looking back. It's only possible when you are an idiot like me who will listen to a guy like you hour after hour, for months, listening to lies like songs on the radio.

The next part is when I stopped being a mother. I agreed to give a deposition about where Rex had been the days before the arrest, which was actually nowhere I knew. The truth was that he'd taken off without explanation or phone calls for three days, which was normal for Rex. He turned up that Saturday afternoon, without his Corvette, dropped off by a friend he'd been helping set up a restaurant in the city, he said. This was when he asked to borrow our car the next morning. His lawyer said that this little deposition from me was the last thing Rex needed to make sure he didn't take part of the fall for Luke. It was, Carol said, the least I could do given the circumstances. So despite the fact that I had on the same day found out that Rex had a police record that included fraud and multiple drug charges, I gave the depo-sition. And when the lawyers and the DA and Rex then told me that I needed to convince Luke to plead guilty and get a reduced sentence, I did that, too.

They told me that even though Luke was eighteen and not a minor, he would only get a slap on the wrist because it was his first offense, that it wouldn't affect his scholar-ship or his life in any way. Do you think I bothered to check with anyone—Stanford, his coach, another lawyer—to see if they knew what they were talking about? Of course I didn't. I listened to Rex. And instead of hiring a decent lawyer and letting a jury decide, I convinced Luke to go along with the plea that they all wanted from him. He was terrified by this point, in jail for days, and the DA spooked him with threats of spending all of his twenties behind bars. The public defender told Luke it was his best shot at a normal life, and in the end he pled guilty. He pleaded guilty and spent eleven months in prison.

What happened next won't surprise you. Rex got off scot-free and in three weeks was gone. No good-bye, no phone call, no note, no thank-you. Nothing. I never saw or heard from him again. I'll bet you saw that part coming, Winton. That part in the story when the dumb woman does or gives the guy who can make her laugh the thing he wants and then he disappears. You've heard that part of the story before. You've heard it and seen it and done it a thousand times.

Did I tell you a woman came to my door tonight and hit me in the face? She did. You probably know her father. Another dumb sucker like me sending money to strangers. At least he's lucky enough to have a daughter to step in. Which she did. She let me have it. And thank God. She knocked some sense into me. Finally, someone knocked some goddamned sense into me! You know what she said? She said I destroyed people's lives and she was right. She told me I had to stop, Winton. She told me to stop, and right now, even though it's too late to do anyone any good, I'm stopping.

Before Winton speaks, Lydia stands up from the kitchen table. She drops the receiver from her ear and hugs it to her chest for a few seconds before carefully returning it to its cradle. Upstairs, the television has been turned off, and for the first time all evening her apartment is silent.

Silas

It has been nine months since he ditched his bike here and snuck down the driveway and across the lawn to the house. Like on that night, there is now a bright moon, not quite full, but nearly so. It lights the road and, opposite the chained driveway entrance, acres of apple and pear orchards where Silas and his friends spent many hours as kids. In the bluish light he pictures Ethan and Charlie whipping apples from long sticks into the stone walls and watching them explode. How many afternoons had they spent there smashing fruit and laughing their heads off? He remembers the Mexican workers who would wave at them and let them be. No one ever seemed to miss those apples or care that they were trespassing. When was the last time they came here? Silas wonders. Two summers ago? Three? It seems like another life-time. Something shines in the dark across the road, and at first he can't tell what it is, but as he steps closer, he sees it's June Reid's old mailbox, dented and silver and still standing. It leans to the left, and the red metal flag points toward the ground. He turns back toward the top of the driveway and descends slowly.

There is no house now, just a dark rectangle of dirt and rock. He sees no sign of anything burned or charred, no sign of what had been here. Its size surprises Silas. It does not look large enough to have once held rooms and furniture and all the complicated systems that keep a house operating. He approaches where the kitchen window would have been and stares into the air above the strange patch of earth. It looks like a garden, he thinks, waiting to be planted, or an enormous grave, freshly dug and filled. He hears a twig snap, and when he jumps to look behind him he sees what is left of the small stone shed, half-lit in moonlight like a ragged ghost. The small cedar shingle roof is mostly burned off but the walls and door remain. Impossibly, two of the boxes of Ball jars are still stacked there. He steps inside, sits down on the dirt floor, and leans back on the cold stone.

Nine months ago, he'd come back here because he had no choice. He tries to remember how late exactly it was, but that part is fuzzy. He knows he got home from work by eight o'clock, because he ate dinner with his parents and sisters. He remembers them needling him about the wedding preparations and the rehearsal dinner at the house. What he'd seen, what he'd heard, who was there. He couldn't understand why all the interest, especially from his mother, who kept asking if he'd seen Luke's mom, Lydia. She'd always had a problem with her. *Did she wear one of her little, low-cut dresses like she used to turn up in at the*

Tap? His sister Gwen yelled, *Mom! That's not nice!* His father laughed and it went on from there.

After eating the vanilla ice-cream bar his mother gives him for dessert, he gets up from the table to go to his room, impatient to pack a hit and crash to sleep. Halfway up the stairs, something seems off. He stops midstair, thinks. The knapsack. Where is it? His chest tightens. Did he just leave it at the kitchen table? He bolts down the stairs into the kitchen and tries to act casual as he sails past the table to the kitchen sink. *Glass of water,* he preemptively mumbles as he scans beneath the table and sees nothing anywhere near where he was sitting. Before getting trapped in conversation, he disappears upstairs and into his room, where he thinks through each beat of the afternoon. He had his knapsack when he and Ethan and Charlie were fucking around and getting high on the Moon. He remembers rushing back and stashing it in the stone shed behind boxes of Ball jars so it was out of sight and off his back while they hurried through the remaining work.

It hits him. *IT'S STILL THERE.* Behind the box, in the shed, next to the house. The fucking knapsack is still there, and in it his bong, his pot, his learner's permit, his school ID, and his cash. An army of people will be showing up first thing in the morning to empty that shed and set up the wedding reception. Rick Howland, the caterer, for one, is definitely going to be there before eight, and Luke is up at six most mornings, so even if he thought about beating Rick to the house, Luke would no doubt be walking the property, picking up sticks, and cursing his half-assed workers for doing such a lame job.

Silas sits on his bed and tries to regulate his breathing. He's crashing from being on his feet and high all afternoon, and he feels like he's hyperventilating. He balls his fists into the top of his thighs, takes a deep breath, and wishes he could go to sleep. But there is no way around the grim truth: he has to go back. He has to ride back up Wildey Road and down along Indian Pond after everyone in his house—and hopefully by then in June Reid's house, too—is asleep.

Which is exactly what he does. Three long hours later, after he's heard the last toilet flush down the hall in his parents' bathroom. After he's jerked off twice and slammed a warm Red Bull that he'd forgotten to drink a few days ago. He's not sure if it's the caffeine or the adrenaline, but as sleepy as he was before, he's now awake. He's ready to get this over with. He steps as softly as he can down the stairs, through the kitchen, and out the back door to where his bike is leaning against the house. He flies down Wildey and Indian Pond and almost overshoots June Reid's driveway. He skids to a stop, gets off his bike, and throws it in the weeds.

From the road, the house is dark. It is an old, two-story stone house, but the far right section, the oldest, is made of wood, and the only windows in front are on the first floor. People could be awake upstairs and from the road he wouldn't know. He'd have to sneak down alongside the kitchen before he'd be able to tell. He considers coming from around the back of the house, but thinks about the noise he'd make trudging through the woods to get there. Better to go quietly down the driveway and slip up the side between the kitchen and the stone shed.

The gravel drive crunches beneath his feet even though he is stepping as gently and slowly as possible. It takes what feels like hours to get to the lawn, where his footfalls are nearly silent. By the time he reaches the near corner of the house, he can see a yellow panel of light hitting the stone shed. The kitchen light is on, and by the way it flickers and wobbles, there must be someone in there. *FUCK FUCK FUCK,* he whispers to him-self. He leans against the side of the house and holds the rough wood siding for balance. He cannot go back now. He will inch along the outside and secure a place next to the kitchen window until whoever is in there goes to sleep. He begins to move. What must be a bat flaps the air just above his head, and he collapses to the ground and covers his face. It takes every bit of control he can muster not to scream. He stays down, adjusts his crouch to a seated position, and crab-crawls gradually to a spot out of the light's path, just to the left of the window. He rests his head against the side of the house and waits. At first no sounds come from inside. The cicadas are everywhere, their sound enormous, but after a while it becomes ambient noise, as elemental and invisible as the dark he is huddled in. Then he hears voices coming from the back of the house. *The fucking screened-in porch,* he thinks, having forgotten until now that it's right there, just behind the kitchen at the back of the house. He's only half the width of the house away. If he sneezes, whoever is in there will hear it. He begins to panic. He's too exposed, too close. If he attempts to leave now, they will hear him. He tries to control his breathing, but focusing on it makes it sound louder, more erratic. He holds his legs in his arms and squeezes. He is only twenty or so yards from the stone shed where his knapsack is, but it might as well be on the other side of town. He is trapped. There is nothing to do but wait for everyone in the house to go to sleep.

Crouching in the dark, he tries to make out what the voices on the porch are saying. It does not sound like people celebrating the night before a wedding. At the wedding of his oldest sister, Holly, they had a keg on the back porch and everyone stayed up until at least four in the morning. He remembers her fiancé, Andrew, a rich kid from New York whose family has a summer-house in town, and how he had an eight ball of coke. His buddies from college broke into the pool at Harkness to go skinny-dipping. This was last summer, and Silas's sisters wouldn't let him join in. He had to stay at the house watching his parents and uncles get shitfaced and listen to Andrew's parents fight about who was sober enough to drive home. This scene at June Reid's is, by comparison, a funeral. He'd seen Lolly around over the years, and she was hot in a rich hippie-chick kind of way, and the guy she was marrying seemed fine, just a bit of a douche bag and a know-it-all. He heard them talking on the lawn earlier that day. Something about flight times and packing bags. It occurs to Silas that Lolly Reid has probably been on over a hundred airplanes and probably to places he's never heard of. Silas had been on one plane: to Orlando, Florida, with his sisters when he was eleven. Their grandmother met them at the airport, and they spent two days in long lines at Disney World. Silas didn't think Lolly Reid, even as a kid, was the type to go to Disney World.

The porch door creaks open and he hears footsteps. They are coming around the house. Then he sees a man. It's Luke. He's wearing a white Izod shirt and dark pants and walking to the back of the lawn toward the trees. He must be taking a leak, Silas thinks as he watches the white of his shirt hover in the far dark like a ghost. He stays there for what feels like a long time, longer than he'd need to piss. Eventually, he makes his way back toward the house, walking directly toward Silas at first and then veering toward the porch door. The voices kick up but then thcy seem to move into the kitchen. Faintly, he hears footsteps on the stairs, the water in the second-floor bathroom turn on, and a toilet flush. A door shuts and then the house is quiet.

In the kitchen above him he hears the water in the sink run briefly. Cupboard doors shutting. And a slow ticking. *Tick. Tick. Tick.* Luke and June are talking and between the words the ticking. She is saying something about beating a dead horse and he is saying her name. She speaks and he simply repeats her name. It's as if hc is trying to talk someone down from the edge of a building or bridge. *June,* he says, and the ticking stops. She speaks, but Silas cannot hear the words. She is too far from the window. It's stressful, whatever they are talking about, and Silas can tcll by the tones and their volume that it's getting worse. Shadows block the light from the window above him. They are right there, inches from his head. And now he hears every word.

June, he says, *I'm not going to apologize for answering her truthfully. And it's true: I've asked you twice now.*

It's not so simple. You know that. June's voice is strict, like his mother's.

But I don't! Why the fuck is it not simple? I'm missing something here and you need to explain it to me. Silas has never heard Luke sound so upset. At work he can get serious, tense, but not like this.

June's voice fades and Silas can only hear bits but he catches her last words because she shouts them. *Because it can't!*

Luke, still by the window, says, *Can't is a lie and you know it. I love you and you say you love me, and not that I have a lot of good examples, but in my book that means you get married.* His voice has risen to near shouting. Silas can hear June; she says something but she's crossed the kitchen toward the stove and her words are just sound. Sound that ends the conversation, launches Luke across the kitchen and out the back porch. The screen door slaps shut and suddenly Luke is outside, walking swiftly and in a straight line to the back of the lawn, to the field, toward the far tree line, which leads to a maze of trails on the Moon. Silas watches his white shirt glide purposefully into the woods and disappear. He hears movement in the kitchen and then the screen door opens and shuts again. This time it is June, running, not walking, across the lawn, toward the woods. Her blond hair is what Silas sees flash along the same path Luke had taken just a minute before. Against the silver-blue field at night, her hair appears lit by a single beam of moonlight, as if it was following her across a great stage, like a spotlight following a rock star at a concert. When she reaches the dark border where the field meets the woods, she disappears, too.

They are gone, but in their place the ticking, which had stopped minutes ago, resumes. At first he thinks someone else must be in the kitchen. He waits a few seconds and the ticking goes on and there is no movement, no break in the light from the window. Did she leave the stove on? Is that even possible? Slowly, Silas stands. His legs and back are stiff from crouching. He steps to the other side of the window where a garden hose is coiled against the side of the house. He holds the window ledge, steps up to the top of the coiled hose, and hoists himself to see inside the kitchen. No one is there. The stove is on the opposite end to the window Silas is looking through—one of those old ones that rich New Yorkers spend thousands of dollars fixing up because they like the way they look. But this one doesn't look fixed up. There is rust along the bottom and some of the knobs look like they've been replaced with makeshift knobs from other stoves. Silas loses his grip on the ledge and jumps down. His foot lands on the hose nozzle and his ankle twists and he collapses awkwardly on the lawn. He stays down. Again, he hears the ticking. *Tick . . . Tick . . . Tick . . . Tick.* What the fuck am I supposed to do? he thinks as he looks out to the field for any trace of Luke's shirt or June's hair. He sees nothing but the dark outline of the reception tent looming in the moonlit grass. No one is around, no one can hear. It's time. He holds his breath and lurches across the short distance between the house and the shed. His hands scramble along the door until he feels and frees the iron latch. The door squeaks like a dying cat as it opens, and for a second he pauses to hear if there is movement or sound from inside the house. Nothing. Just the ticking, which has with the new distance from the house almost disappeared into the hum of the cicadas. It is hidden in the noise of the world and heard only if you stop to listen for it. Silas stops listening for it. Still on his knees, he feels behind the stack of Ball-jar boxes for his knapsack, and *YES-HOLY-FUCK-YES* it is there. He slides it around the boxes and holds it like a long-lost and beloved puppy. *Time to go,* he leans down and whispers into the bag, imagining the first hit he will take from his bong once he's cleared the property. He closes the squeaking shed door, folds the latch shut, looks toward the driveway, and pictures his bike hidden in the weeds.

He stands to leave and there it is again, the ticking. *Motherfucking fucker,* he grumbles under his breath. Though it is the last thing on earth he wants to do, he steps toward the house. The closer he gets, the louder the sound. He can't believe the whole house isn't awake by now. He imagines Lolly sleeping and wonders if she is upstairs, alone, the night before her wedding; or if that nerdy douche bag is with her. He wonders if they've fucked tonight or if they're waiting for their honeymoon. Silas hasn't fucked anyone, and so far he hasn't come close. He imagines Lolly upstairs getting fucked, and for a second he thinks he even hears a moan. He steps closer to the house and listens. The only sound he can hear is the ticking, and without thinking his feet move toward it. Soon he is under the window where he stood before, and here the ticking is the loudest. The noise is relentless, louder with each spark. He is the only one who hears.

Cissy

Dad was a looker. Tall guy, big shoulders, eyes as green as grass. Mom never stood a chance. They met when she was fifteen, pulling starfish from the sea or some nonsense. He was eighteen, engaged to marry a girl on the rez, and nine months later, upstairs in this same house, in the room my sister Pam now sleeps in, my sister Helen was born. All five of us were born in that room, up in Mom's bed. And now all five of us, who got married and moved out, have come back, widows or divorcées, or just hopeless, to live here again. The only difference now is Mom's been long dead. Buried in the Moclips cemetery next to her parents and nowhere near Dad, who was buried on the rez. I guess even at fifteen Mom knew what she wanted. She wanted Dad, and even though she couldn't have him, she did. The story goes that when Dad went to his parents to tell them he'd knocked up a white girl from town, they didn't bat an eyelash or raise their voices or hands to him. They moved fast and got him married within the month to that poor girl on the rez he was already engaged to. And that, as Mom used to say, was that. He had a son with that wife, and five daughters with Mom. Mom stayed with Gramma and Granpa and the three of them raised us. Dad came by for lunches a few times a week. Never at night, always in the day. We'd line up like little girl soldiers awaiting inspection when he walked in. He'd give us kisses and butterscotch candies and ask us about school and boys and wink before sitting down for a sandwich and coffee and cigarettes in the kitchen with Mom.

Mom graduated from Moclips High School and went to Grays Harbor College and got an associate degree. She was pregnant on and off through most of that schooling time, and she always said she never minded the gossip. She had Dad and Gramma and Granpa and us, she said, and besides, it kept the boys away. She would have kept going in school but Grays only gives out a two-year degree and nothing else was close enough for her to go to classes and come home in the same day. She worked as an assistant librarian at the public library in Ocean Shores until she died in 2000. Dad died that same year. His wife is still alive and lives on the rez. She must be in her eighties, maybe older. She survived her husband and her son, who died not so long ago, and she lives, like me, with what's left of her family. My sisters and I never had a problem with any of them, but we were always careful to steer clear. We knew no one there wanted anything to do with us and we stayed away. For the most part, we still do.

I've been on the reservation five times in my

life, and three of those times were because of Will
Landis. This last time was to let folks there know
that he'd died. He was not one of them, but he
got under everyone's skin over there, and I knew
they'd want to know. That boy got under a lot of
our skins whether we wanted him to or not. He
was the kid of a couple of hippies from Portland
who moved here in the early nineties to teach
elementary school. They moved into the house
Ben built us after we got married, same house he
died in. I had no reason to stay on in the place, so
my sister Pam sold it and I walked a few doors
down to live with my sisters. I was the last one to
come home, which made sense being that I'm
the youngest. Will was the youngest, too, but that
wasn't what got to me about him. What got to me
was that he worked. Tell him to paint a barn and
he'd find the paint and brush and he'd do it until
it was done. Tell him to clean the sea of seaweed
and he'd run and get a rake. That kid didn't
blink, and the only other person I ever knew like
that was Ben. So I let Will tag along. He came
knocking on my door ready for work, and work I
gave him. From ten to four and for a buck a day.
The Hillworths didn't like it at first. I think they
thought they'd get fined by the state for exploiting
a minor, but the kid made himself useful and
got under their skins, too. He'd wash their old
Ford wagon, bundle their newspapers and magazines and haul them out for recycling, run up to

the hardware store or Laird's for anything and everything. I'm telling you he was Ben, but a boy and a tenth as tall. Nothing to say about Ben but that he woke early, came home late, worked hard, slept deep, and was true-blue. He was the one for me, and the only thing he ever did wrong was smoke and it killed him. I never thought I'd want anyone around like I did Ben, so the whole thing was a fluke to begin with. His leaving was less a surprise than his showing up in the first place, so after he died I just kept going and went back to plan A, which was the house I grew up in, with my sisters. And that's when that Landis kid showed up. Ten years old and living with those hippies who didn't know the first thing about keeping a house going. He'd come knocking each morning to go to work and keep going until I said so.

After I heard Will had died, I walked down Pacific Avenue to the rez. Thing was, that Landis kid also got under the skin of Joe Chenois. He was a leader, someone who fought to get back stolen land for the Quinault. The one time I ever asked him a favor was to give the Landis kid a shot. He was done cleaning gutters and stripping sheets and hauling trash at the Moonstone and was ready for something else. He never shut up about the rez and was itching to find out as much as he could. So I went down to Joe's office and asked him to put him to work, and before long the whole place was calling him Little Cedar. He loved it there and he worshipped Joe. All of them over there did. Tall, like Dad. Had his green eyes, too. Will still came by a few times a week to help out at the Moonstone, or he'd come by the house and barge up the front stairs full of stories from the rez: how Joe had scored some victory against the state, what the carvers who made the old canoes charged tourists for a paddle up the beach. Those old boys loved to tell him the legends and myths of the tribe, and he sucked it all up like a sponge. He'd get extra excited about the stories involving the spit of sand between here and the rez that used to be a camp for the young Quinault girls who'd come of age but were not yet married. The old-timers still say mermaids protected them from men or whatever else might harm them. Anyone who's grown up around here has heard these stories a thousand times. But the way Will told them opened my ears. He loved every inch of this place. He couldn't get enough of the people here and their history, and though I'd spent most of my life avoiding the rez and the shaming eyes of the tribe, I liked to hear his version of it.

Just before he went East to college, he talked me into going down to the rez to see a canoe he'd worked on. After four years and a mess of help from Joe and the carvers, he'd done it. I had no intention of going when he first brought it up in

May, but by August he'd worn me down, and I agreed to walk down the beach with him one evening after work. I could hear Joe coughing before we entered the long woodshed. I hadn't heard coughing like that—the kind that sounds like lungs ripping apart—since Ben. Joe was around my age, but standing in the bright work lights of the woodshed he looked twenty years older, stooped, his skin wrinkled and dry. I could see a pack of Camels bulging from his shirt pocket. *You got quite a boy,* he said, greeting me as he always had: friendly, cautious. *He's not mine* was what I think I said. Joe smiled and shook his head and half whispered, *We had no say in the matter.*

He coughed, pointing to the only canoe in the shed, propped up on sawhorses and at least thirty feet long. *How do you like that?* I could see it was a traditional Quinault—long and wide and carved from a single cedar log. It had a high prow and a low, snug stern, with four cedar planks crossing the middle. I remember Dad telling us stories of how it could take as long as two years to make a canoe like this. How the master carvers would chisel the shell, and to seal it, they'd fill it with water and drop in burning rocks to make it boil. They'd then let it sit through the winter and spring to season. I hadn't thought of him telling us those stories in a long time. I walked around the back to the prow and could see that every inch of the boat's outside had been painted. I couldn't make out the design right away, but as I got closer to the prow, I could see the face of a woman on one side and the face of a man on the other. Both had long, silver hair that flowed from the prow to the stern in waves that looked like the sea. In the waves were green fish, black whales, and blue and gold mermaids. Neither face was recognizable, but I knew. Joe came up beside me and put his arm around my shoulders. In all our years we never so much as held hands. Even at our father's funeral we kept our distance, just as we had our whole lives.

Joe died a year later. Another good man who smoked himself to death. Will came home from college and we went together to the memorial. Some folks on the rez had always looked at me sideways, and I'm sure a few did that day when I showed up with Little Cedar. But it's none of my business. My sisters didn't go, just like they didn't go to our dad's funeral. Not because they didn't love him, but the truth was that, for us, Dad existed in our kitchen and no place else. He was like a handsome neighbor who dropped in and lit the place for a few hours and left. The rez was his world, his people, and though he never said so, we weren't welcome there. Still, I went to Dad's funeral because Ben insisted, and I'm glad I did. Just like I'm glad I went to Joe's. He was a hero on the rez and a thorn in the side of anyone who tried to keep from the Quinault what he believed was theirs. Hundreds of people turned up, and Will, among many others, said a few words. I was proud to watch him stand up before the people I avoided my whole life and tell them how Joe always had time for him, and how by example he taught him to want the kind of life he lived, the useful kind.

Ben and I didn't have kids. We never tried but we never tried not to, either. It just didn't happen and I don't think about it much. But that once-in-a-blue-moon wonder about what kind we might have had came up as one by one people stood and spoke their good words. I knew Joe was a leader and someone people looked up to, but I was surprised to see how many lives one man could affect. You could say I felt proud. Of Joe, of Will, of myself for pointing them at each other. But more than that I missed Ben and wished he were next to me, listening to Will speak about Joe. I don't waste time wanting things to be different than they are. But on that day it hurt how much I wished Ben had stayed around long enough to know the only boy I would have been proud to call mine.

The world's magic sneaks up on you in secret, settles next to you when you have your head turned. It can appear as a tall boy who smells like fish who pulls your braid one night in a bar and asks you to marry him. Or it can be a kid who shows up on your doorstep. Will didn't show up empty-handed, and he didn't go without leaving something behind. Not only did he give me a little bit of Ben when I was missing him the most, and good company that didn't ask for anything but chores to do and to be nearby, but when I wasn't looking, he tricked me into remembering half of who I am.

When the invitations for Will's wedding came, I checked the box that said regrets and mailed it back the next day. He knew I wasn't flying on some plane across the country. But I was happy he'd found someone. He brought her here their first summer to show her where he was from. I made them soup and we walked the beach and I listened to the waves as he told his love the old stories of mermaids and magic. Unlike most people, Will didn't bend a tale or make it more with each telling. He told each one to her as Joe told them to him when he was a boy, just as Dad told them to me.

After Will died, I expected I'd run through all the surprises. That everyone who would play a part or turn up would have done so by then. I settled in and did my bit at work and at home, and that, I thought, was that. And then a woman who called herself Jane checked into Room 6. And she stayed.

Silas

It is winter and there are no cicadas, but he hears them. He crouches next to the boxes of Ball jars, his back to the stone shed, and he hears the night frogs. They sound wild, tropical. It is cold but he can remember the warm air, the too-bright moon. He is where he was. And everyone is as they were, everything is still intact. He can see and hear it all. The words, the porch door, Luke's white shirt glowing across the field, June following behind.

The ticking hasn't stopped. He wonders again if there is anyone else in the house. Is it possible Lolly is alone? How can she not hear it? How can anyone sleep through something so fucking loud? He pictures her topless, wearing only panties, sleeping above the covers. He imagines her skin— perfect, glowing—not like the girls from town who seem less protected from the elements. *WAKE THE FUCK UP!* he thinks and almost shouts. The ticking continues and there is no sound of movement in the house. He scans the field and tree line for signs of Luke and June, but there are none. Someone has to turn off the stove, and he knows there is no one but him. It will just take a second, he tells himself. He'll be in and out before Luke and June are back and without anyone in the house knowing. Just a twist of the knob and it will be okay. He won't get caught. If he left now, who knows what could happen. He's heard stories of houses filling with gas and with the flip of a light switch blowing a mile high. But aren't these just stories parents tell their kids to scare them into being careful? *Shit,* he mutters under his breath, and starts to move slowly along the side of the house. He inches quietly to the porch door, opens it as carefully as he can, and steps through. He crosses the porch and takes two cautious steps up the slate stairs into the house. He stands at the foot of the dark stairway that leads to the second floor. He dares himself to look along the railing, up. There is no sound there, no movement. No one has heard him. The ticking is louder than the sound of his feet on the wide-plank wood floors, and he times each step to coincide with the beat of the stove's threat. He steps up to the old white devil and looks down into the burner and sees the little hammer tap without sparking each time it ticks. No markings are on the stove or the dial to tell him which is off and which is on. No words are on the stove anywhere. He tries the knob closest to the burner and without thinking turns it to the left. It ticks once, and right away a small explosion of flames billows before him with a whoosh. It is nothing more than a flash, and just as quickly as it explodes, the flames recede to a few inches. The ticking stops. He turns it back to the right and the flame goes out. He stands there, rattled by the burst but relieved the ticking has stopped. And then it starts again. *What the fuck* he whispers, scanning the burner, the knob. He turns it to the left again and the ticking stops and this time there is no flame. Maybe it was just because so much gas had built up before. Maybe that's why when he turned it off there was a flame. It just needed to burn through. He's suddenly confused and he wishes he'd never got out of bed that morning, never worked for Luke that day, never smoked pot on the Moon and lost track of time, never left his fucking knapsack behind in the shed. He looks at the stove for answers and there are none. The ticking has stopped but it doesn't make sense that the stove is off. He thinks he smells gas but isn't sure. If there is gas, it must be lingering from before. Or is it? He didn't smell it when he came in. He's sweating now, his hands are slick. He closes his eyes, thinks. It has stopped ticking so it must be off. He tries to think through all the movements —left, right, left. Or was it right, left, right? Didn't the flame go on when he turned it to the left? How could that be off if he had to turn it back to where it was? Or did he? He blinks his eyes a few times, roughs his hair, and tries to focus again on what just happened. He hears a floorboard upstairs and knows he has to get out of the house. It's stopped ticking, he reasons one last time, so it's off. Before he leaves, he looks around the kitchen. It is bright, and as old as the stove is, the other appliances are new, sleek. Thick slabs of white marble are on the counters, and below the window is a deep double sink with a high, curving faucet. The cabinets are painted pale yellow, the walls white. He takes one last look at the stove, sniffs for gas again, and this time is sure he smells it, but just a trace. On the counter he sees a pair of cat-eyed sunglasses he saw Lolly wearing when she was talking to what must have been her fiancé's family in the lawn that afternoon. He moves toward them, but before he reaches the counter, he hears a door open upstairs and then footsteps. All at once he is moving, across the kitchen, down into the screened porch, toward the door. He knocks against a wicker chair and it skids a few feet across the slate. As quickly as he can, he gently lifts it back into position, symmetrical with the couch and opposite another chair. As he lowers the chair to the floor, he notices the tossed white and blue cushions, a soft beige blanket folded over the low arm of the sofa, scattered candles, extinguished now, their wax melted down, wicks black. He knows he should hurry but something holds him there. The just-used space, the lingering smell of citronella and perfume, the dimpled cushions where people had only minutes before been sitting. He remembers Luke's mom and June

Reid there earlier, laughing. A toilet flushes upstairs and he steps back, turns away, and leaves through the porch door, which he accidentally lets bang behind him. He lunges for his knapsack, which he'd left next to the shed, sprints across the front lawn, up the dark driveway, and onto the road. He fetches his bike from the weeds, curls the knapsack over his shoulder, and tightens the straps to his chest. He swings one leg over the bike and grips the handlebars. His hands are shaking. *I'm going,* he mutters, confirming and challenging what is happening, what should probably not be happening. He toes the left pedal and imagines the first blessed hit. The tires begin to roll on the asphalt beneath him. He feels the bong shift in the knapsack behind him. *I'm going,* he says again, this time convinced.

He pedals furiously until he's passed the church and turned left onto an old, unused logging road. He can practically taste the smoke in his mouth as he jumps off the bike, unzips his knapsack, and lunges for the bong. His arms are still shaking. *What the fuck just happened?* he mumbles to himself, remembering the smell of gas. *What did I do?*

He thinks, briefly, of going back, calling upstairs into the sleeping house to wake Lolly or anyone who will listen. He considers this as he packs his bowl with thick pinches of pot and fishes in the front pocket of his knapsack for a lighter. He settles down in the grass next to his bike and crosses his legs, Indian style. He runs through the consequences—the police, his parents, Luke. He pulls the bong toward his lap, leans forward, and as he slowly fills his lungs, his mind empties. He holds off exhaling for as long as he can, and when he does, pot smoke curls around his head and dances above him like ghost flames. He closes his eyes and pulls his knees toward his chest. The preceding hours, minute by agonizing minute, become less urgent, gradually vanish. He smokes another hit. His body calms, he exhales, and the world is, again, simple: the humming cicadas, the spark of a lighter, and the sound of one boy breathing.

June

Lolly was right. The Moonstone sits at the edge of the world. June has driven as far as she can and this is where she will stop. In this room with white walls and gray carpet and a golden mermaid painted on a piece of driftwood hung above the bed. She will stay here for as long as she needs to, maybe forever, she thinks as she switches the light off and lays her head on the pillow. She hears the ocean outside, pounding the shore, over and over, and for the first time she allows herself to remember that night, does not will it away.

She is standing at the sink, filling the kettle for tea, but she is already boiling. About something that has sat unbudging and blunt between them since New Year's Eve when he asked her to marry him. She'd responded by laughing; evading the question by pretending he was joking, as if he'd suggested they cross the field behind their house, march up the steps of the main building at the Unification Church, and join the Moonies. Her laugh that night was so dismissive and distant, so effective, that it took him almost a month to bring it up again. He'd built a fire and they were eating bowls of risotto she'd made, left over from the night before when Lydia was over for dinner. She'd asked about Lolly's wedding in May. Lolly had called after Thanksgiving to tell June she and Will would accept her nearly-a-year-on-the-table offer to have the reception at the house. This now gave them less than six months to rent a tent, June explained, mail invitations, hire a caterer, organize flowers, and all the rest of it. June noticed Luke get quiet around the talk of wedding plans, but he didn't say anything after Lydia left. He waited until the next night and asked if June's hesitation had to do with money and the great difference in their circumstances. He was making a decent living with his landscaping business, but he could not compete with what she had in the bank and the house, which had been paid off when she was still married to Adam. He said if that was her concern, he was happy to sign any prenup or contract she wanted. She can't say the idea of a prenup hadn't crossed her mind since he'd proposed; it had, but barely. The truth was, she hadn't considered the option of marrying him seriously enough to think through the financial or legal consequences. The only consequence that flashed through June's mind on New Year's Eve, when Luke bent down on one knee and held out an unusual and pretty pink enamel ring, was Lolly. It had only been a few years now that she'd been communicating with her. Less than two since she would even acknowledge Luke's existence and speak his name. Only a few weeks since she'd accepted June's offer to have the wedding reception at the house. To barge into all this with the news that she and Luke were getting married would only confirm her fundamental theory about June: that she thought of herself first and foremost and only, and that her actions never took into account the impact they'd have on others, especially Lolly. This is what June thought that night as she tried to make up for her insensitive first response, tried to assure Luke that this was not something they needed to worry about. She did not explain her reasons because instinctively she did not want to pit Luke against Lolly. Position Lolly between Luke and what he wanted. She had finally convinced Lolly to give Luke a chance and did not want to risk his resenting her. But she did not say any of this that night in front of the fire in February. She also did not say she'd laughed when he proposed because she was caught off guard and because it was impossible. What she said was that she loved him and for now that had to be enough. And for that night, and a while after, it was. She kept the ring in its gray box in the top drawer of her dresser with the rest of her jewelry. She told him it was too large, that she would have it sized at a shop in Salisbury; but in truth the ring fit perfectly and she had no intention of wearing it. Not because she didn't think it was beautiful—it was, in its particular, vintage art deco way—but because she did not want to be wearing the open question on her finger, waving it between them daily. What she wanted was for the question itself to go away.

But tonight the question has returned, and her response is much worse than before. She is frozen at the stove, one hand in a fist on her hip, the other holding the knob that produces no spark, no flame. Luke has just left, and behind him the door to the screened porch has just slammed. With words she can't recognize, she has driven him away. She fiddles with the knob, twists it all the way left again and waits for the stove to light, but instead there is only the faint smell of gas. *Oh, shit,* she mutters, thinking the pilot might have gone out again. It was so hard to tell with this stove. Sometimes it would light right away, explode in a fireball, or it would take forever or not at all. She turns the dial all the way right, off, and as usual it sparks—once, twice, again, again . . . It will quit after a few minutes, or maybe longer, but eventually the ticking will stop. It's been like this for years. She will replace this heap, she swears to herself every time it fails to light, like now, and keeps ticking long after the burner has been turned off. She will replace it when she fixes the torn screen on the porch and the broken dryer downstairs, but not until after the wedding, not until things settle down. She leaves the stove and rushes through the porch door and out toward the lawn. She pauses to let her eyes adjust, for the blank dark to fill with the shapes of trees, shed, field, tent. Near the far tree line at the back of the field, she can see the bright smudge of Luke's white shirt above the tall grass. She runs toward it.

On the mown path along the edge of the field she follows his figure to the woods, where it disappears off the nearest trailhead. The moon is nearly full, and the field, the woods, the far-off Berkshires, are lit with a silver light, as if the world were an exposed negative. By the time she steps onto the trail that leads to the Unification Church property, she's lost him. She scans for any flash of Luke's shirt and calls out his name as she goes, careful not to trip on a root or rock on the path. She follows the trail they have walked together a thousand times and remembers again the night he asked her to marry him, how unprepared she was for the question and how relieved she was to derail the prospect, at least for a little while. There was no one else she wanted to be with, but even beyond the issues with Lolly the idea of marrying again was difficult to engage. Prenups, the fear that he would resent her for not being able to give him children, the embarrassment of their age difference, the memory of her bitter divorce with Adam—all these things would crowd in and it would be impossible to imagine.

For an hour she follows the path—through the woods, along the back lawn of the Unification Church, and down the road that circles back to the side field of her property. Even in the moonlit night, she cannot find him. She steps into the field and can see across it to the dark mass that is her house and the silhouette of the great white tent that has been assembled for the wedding reception tomorrow. It looks like a giant dog curled at the foot of the house, guarding her sleeping family. She starts to cross the field and stops when she hears a twig snap behind her. She calls Luke's name and walks back onto the trail a few yards in and calls again. An owl sounds a muffled taunt in response. *Fool. Fool. Fool.*

She leaves the woods and slowly makes her way along the mown path toward the lawn, listening behind her as she goes. She reaches the tent and looks back before stepping inside. She scans the eerie, silver-tinted field and the trees beyond, but does not see Luke.

She steps inside the tent toward the end of one of the three long reception tables not yet set with china and flowers. She sits down on one of the wooden folding chairs and thinks of the clamor and laughter that will fill this space tomorrow and remembers her wedding to Adam twenty-three years ago. She was pregnant with Lolly but no one, not even Adam knew. She had not taken a test nor seen a doctor yet, but she knew, and she remembered thinking she now had what she needed from a husband: a child—and therefore could disappear and start her life over with her son or her daughter and not have to go through with all of the rest of it. She hadn't thought of that night or her escape fantasy in over twenty years. It had never occurred to her before now to imagine what it would be like to be married to someone who had these thoughts the night before her wedding. She wonders if Adam registered her ambivalence then and for the first time considers how those feelings might have set an early course for what would later play out in their marriage. She wonders if Lolly is having the same thoughts now, lying awake beside her husband-to-be, plotting a secret flight before dawn. Not likely. But then who would have imagined anything that June was thinking all those years ago; on the surface she was a giddy bride marrying her college love, continuing a life in New York that seemed blessed. Still, deep down she knew it was more likely to fall apart than succeed. She knew, but she smothered that knowing with the future that everyone in her life saw for them and that she could, through their eyes, occasionally see. Her father was struggling with a bad heart then and her mother died when she was in college, so there was also, she remembers now, a feeling of needing to be anchored, placed in the world.

She experiences an unfamiliar mix of compassion and resentment when she thinks of Adam sleeping upstairs in the house. She remembers Lolly insisting he spend the weekend with them and is grateful she eventually backed away from that fight. It escalated quickly the day before he came, and after a sharp exchange and a long walk in the woods, it became clear that if she insisted Adam stay at the Betsy, where she'd booked him a room, the weekend would be ruined and it would demolish all progress she and Lolly had made and sabotage the chance for more. And Lolly was right. Adam's being around had been easy and felt strangely comfortable. She cringes as she thinks how close she came to drawing the line and refusing, what the fallout would have been. She holds her head in her hands and squeezes.

She sees Luke. Months ago, on one knee, proposing; the pink enamel ring wedged in its gray velvet box, the destroyed look in his eyes when she laughed. His confused and beautiful face tonight when he stood in the kitchen and asked, plainly and without anger, *Why?* What she said next came not from anything she believed or meant but what she imagined others saying, what she feared her friends in the city snickered behind her back, and the small-town gossips murmured at the grocery store. What she said held all the agitation she felt because the evening with Lolly had ended on a sour note, because the subject of Luke and June's getting married had come up at all, and because Luke hadn't just simply brushed it off and restored ease. What she said next were words she would do anything to retrieve. *Because you're not the guy someone like me marries, you're the guy someone like me ends up with after their marriage is over.* She heard the words for the first time as she said them, had not thought them through, considered or uttered them to herself before, under her breath or out loud. She saw them fly and hit their target, and as he stormed away, she turned the dial on the stove to the right, off, and with the slam of the screen door and the riot of tree frogs and cicadas outside, the ticking began.

She pulls her legs toward her chest and positions her tennis shoes on the edge of the folding chair and looks up into the billowing silver-white tent. She rocks, slowly, feeling the guilty, shameful bruise of being wrong spread across her chest and up her neck to her face. How could she be so cruel to a man who had only ever offered her friendship and kindness and love? She knows the only way he will ever forgive her, the only hope they could have after what she has said is for her to simply say yes. To marry him. She is fifty-two; Luke is thirty. They have known each other for three years, and never has he been dishonest or unkind. Careless, maybe. Selfish, yes. Impatient, sometimes. But he has been more of a partner to her than Adam ever was, and she trusts him. And unlike Adam, who avoided her physically after Lolly was born, Luke found ways to touch her all through the day. His fingers would often brush across the top of her arms, his hands constantly palming her backside when she crossed in front of him. And the sex, though more frequent than she might have preferred, was often as emotionally overwhelming as it was physically surprising. His body, in clothes and out, still shocked her, and touching him could send her into girlish fits of giggling or silence her completely. Why should she let her past and her pride stop her from giving him what he wants? What she wants. She stretches her legs and places her feet on the chair in front of her. She breathes in the still night air and feels the muscles in her shoulders and neck loosen as she exhales. There it is, she thinks to herself, remembering a similar feeling of relief when she decided to leave Adam. She remembers, too, how after she'd made the decision she looked back on the preceding years of her marriage—all the doubt and lies and clues—and wondered why it took so long to do what was suddenly so obvious. These were the questions then and the questions now. Why were some decisions so tortured and then not? Why has she only ever learned the most important lessons at the speed of great pain?

She pulls her jacket across her chest and settles into the two folding chairs she's made into a makeshift bed. She will wait for him to come back. She will stay out here in the summer night, with the deer sneezing in the woods and the frogs chirping from the trees. She will wait for him here. Under this wedding tent, she will wait. And she will say yes.

Silas

It is after three in the morning by the time he has pedaled back to town. He has not taken a hit since just after Lydia Morey stood on the sidewalk screaming at him. There will be no more hits tonight since his bong is now reduced to a pile of broken glass rattling in his knapsack. But for once he doesn't want to be high. For once he doesn't want anything between him and the world. He's tired, and it is time. But before doing what he knows he should have done months ago, he needed to go back, retrace his steps, and remember it clearly enough to tell. He remembers Luke telling the three of them he needed them to work twice as hard that day. *You're good,* he said. *But today I need great.* He remembers bolting with Ethan and Charlie to the back field as soon as Luke was out of the driveway, fucking around on the Moon and rushing through the remaining work when they got back. Luke must have seen the shitty job when he got home. He would have said something when he saw them next, but he wouldn't have blown up or been an asshole. He would just have said he needed better than they gave, and if they couldn't clean up their act, he'd have to find other guys. He'd said it before and it usually made them feel guilty enough to kick ass for a month or so and get back in his good graces. He remembered how Luke was an adult but didn't seem like one. They feared him a little but mainly they respected him. Physically, for one—no one they knew was stronger; but he was responsible without being an asshole. Worked hard without being a dick. Every once in a while, when they'd be working on a job with him, he'd get mad at something he'd done and throw a shovel, or one time he broke a rake across his knee. But these outbursts didn't happen often and they weren't directed at the guys who worked for him. Luke was a good guy. Not the druggie Silas's mother made him out to be when she first refused to let him work for Luke. But when no other jobs came up that summer between eighth grade and his freshman year in high school, she caved in. Still, she warned Silas she was keeping an eye out and to watch out for what she called screwy business. There was never any screwy business, and after a while the stories of jail and drug dealing seemed like they must have been about someone else. They made no sense with the guy he'd worked for on and off since he was thirteen. But his mother never backed down, never allowed for the possibility that she or any of the other gossips in town were wrong. And then the accident happened and she had what she needed. *I'm sorry, but I knew something would go wrong over there,* she said the same day it all happened. *You can only fool people for so long. I'm just glad Silas didn't get wrapped up in it.* He remembers his mother on the phone that day. How it only took minutes before she was spreading stories, coming up with a cause and a culprit. But what he remembers most sharply is that he said nothing to stop her or any of the other people who cracked jokes, embellished rumors, or passed judgment. What he remembers is saying nothing. What he remembers is seeing Lydia Morey at the coffee shop a few months after everything happened and wanting, right then, to go up to her and tell her the truth. He didn't have the guts then, just like he didn't have the guts every time he'd seen her after. Instead, he followed her at a safe distance around town. He's even stood in the driveway outside her apartment building and watched her walk from room to room. Every time he has seen her, he thinks this will be the time he will step out of the shadows, and each time he loses his nerve. Not only because of what it might mean for him, but because he can't imagine not seeing her anymore as he has. Unaware, sad, alone. It would be impossible to explain to someone else, but he thinks of himself as her guardian, her shadow. No one would see it that way, he knows, especially Lydia. And once he says to her what he has to say, he expects he will be the last person on earth she will want to understand. Maybe if he hadn't frightened her tonight things might have stayed the same. He might have stayed her shadow for years. But there is no way he can be invisible to her again. And he can't undo what he's done. If there is one thing he has come to understand this year, it is this.

The town is silent, every light is off besides the streetlamps that light their usual circles. It is late but Silas is awake, and he is not nervous. He steps across the front porch of Lydia's apartment building and knocks on the door. Soon, she is in front of him. She is standing behind the glass window in the door, a gray robe folded across her chest, her hair falling around her face and catching the light from the kitchen behind her. She will not unlock this door, she is saying, but he is not bothered. She will call the police, she warns, but he does not budge. He will wait until she trusts him. He will stay as long as he has to this time. And then he will tell her.

Lydia

The truth will set you free. Funny, she thinks as the flight attendant demonstrates how to buckle the seat belts and breathe through the oxygen mask, how it would take a con artist and a kid destroyed by secrets to set her on this path, put her on an airplane for the first time in her life. *The truth will set you free, dear Lydia,* Winton said in his sing-song way on that last phone call. *Because it is the only thing that can.* He was only trying to engage her in conversation that night, but he nudged to an end what had gone on too long. The truth was something she had hidden or bent all her adult life, and she had suffered and caused others to suffer because of it. Silas, that poor tortured boy, showed her by telling the truth that this was no longer a life she could live. Silas, who she at first wanted to strangle for being so stupid, for making the choice he did to save himself; but as painful and senseless as what he told her might seem to anyone else, she understood. She understood bad choices made from fear, acted on out of a misguided sense of survival. She would never call the police to tell them what he told her. What he did he can never take back, and that will be punishment enough. He'd carried his secret as

269

far as he could and then let it go. It was time she did, too.

She has gathered everything and organized it chronologically in folders wrapped in red rubber bands: report cards, letters to Santa, articles in newspapers about breaking state records, getting the scholarship to Stanford, photographs of shaking hands with the governor, dressed up in a tuxedo for the prom, shirtless on a summer day washing his car. There is, too, the one article in the local paper about Luke's arrest. Why she cut it out at the time and saved it all these years she does not know. But it is folded neatly with the others, the headline *Wells Swim Champ Arrested for Drug Trafficking* above a few short sentences reporting how Luke was taken into custody after more than a pound of cocaine was found in his car and in the apartment he shared with his mother. This, too, she will show to George and explain her part. The only picture of Luke with June is one she took in the parking lot of the church the night of Lolly's wedding rehearsal. She kept the film in her camera until this week, when she walked it to the pharmacy to be developed. Only three pictures were on the roll: two of Will and Lolly and one of Luke and June standing in front of his truck—him smiling into the camera, her serious, distracted by something to the left of the frame. Then there are the articles of what came after, which she printed at the library from the

270

computer. These she did not read or look at, but folded quickly as they spooled from the printer and later tucked in with the rest. It is not everything, but she has gathered as much as she can to tell George the story of their son.

The morning after Silas stood on her front porch, Lydia walked to the library and sat down at a computer to see what she could find. She typed into the Google search box the letters that spelled *George King,* the name on the business card she kept for years and eventually threw away. She kept it through the pregnancy, which she did not expect, but when she found out she was three months along, she knew who the father was. Earl was in a nightly blackout so he had no idea they hadn't had sex in more than six months. No man ever crowed louder when he found out he was going to be a father. She let him carry on, but she held on to that business card, tucked it deep in her wallet, and waited for the storm that was coming. She knew it was going to be rough, that most likely it would be clear to everyone right away that Earl was not the father, but she knew on the other side there was a strong chance she'd be free and she'd have a child. She held on to that card through the expected divorce and the first lonely years after, with no alimony or support of any kind from Earl, no support from anyone but her mother, and even that was at arm's length, with conditions, and scornful.

Many times she almost called that number. But she didn't want to complicate a life she knew was already complicated. Not until Luke started swimming was it clear her baby could do something better than anyone else, was going to be all right on his own someday without his mother, and without the help of a father he never knew. This is when she ripped up the card; the only-in-an-extreme-emergency button she never pushed.

George King. After a few pecked letters on the computer keyboard, she had an address, an obituary for his wife—cancer, eleven years after he'd been in Wells—a business address, and a number, which she later called. After three rings the line clicked to an automated outgoing message, and she listened for an option that would confirm he still worked there. *For George King, press one,* the generic voice spoke. *For Rick King, press two.* Over thirty years later and George King was right where he was then. Working with his brother in Atlanta, Georgia. It seemed too easy to find him. She played the message again and pressed one. She had no intention of speaking to him but wanted to see what would happen. A young Southern woman answered brightly, *George King's office. Hello?* Heart thumping, Lydia immediately hung up. After a few more keystrokes at the library, pictures appeared on the screen. Here was the man she knew for less than three weeks, who asked her questions, listened to the answers, and who was, then, as lost and fearful as she was. He looked much the same, but thicker and balding, gray now dominating what remained of his coarse and closely cut hair and beard. In one of the photos he had won a golf championship at a country club, and another was a group shot of a high school reunion. Both were photos taken in the last three years. It surprised her to see him handsome, tall, and distinguished. He had been, then, in his midthirties, a young father, panicked about the future—money, his wife, his troubled son, his pushy brother—but here he was a successful man nearing retirement. He wore the sort of clothes worn by the men from New York Lydia worked for, and in his eyes was none of the startled and still-clinging youth she remembered. Yet the kindness she found there when she needed it, this she could see. Looking at these few photos, the first glimpses she'd had of George King since that last morning at the Betsy, she could see the same high forehead, wide smile, and thin, almost feminine, eyebrows. Here was Luke if he had grown to late middle age, the man who would have grown old with June and who would some-day, maybe, she thinks for the first time now, have met his father. Lydia's deal with Luke was that she'd tell him when he was twenty-one, and as a kid and in high school it became an every-so-often, light running joke between them. *Denzel's going to want me to change my name to Washington after we meet, right?* he'd joke. *Because that may cost him a few dollars. He's got some years to make up for, don't you think?*

At twenty-one, Luke wasn't interested in anything she had to say, and later, in that first year after June brought them back into each other's lives, they tiptoed around it, were moving cautiously toward the heavy subjects. They were being careful with each other, taking their time. *We'll get there,* Lydia told June once when she'd pressed about it, *but there's no rush now, we have the rest of our lives.*

The day after she called George's office, she called a 1-800 number for American Airlines that she found in the back of a travel magazine at the library and asked for a flight from Hartford, Connecticut, to Atlanta, Georgia. This was the first plane ticket she'd ever purchased, the first time she would travel in anything but a car.

Three days later an envelope with a Washington State postmark arrived in her mailbox. After she opened it and read Mimi Landis's short note on motel stationery to let her know where June was living and the contact details there, she called the airline again. She read her confirmation number over the phone and when she finished asked if she could change the ticket to fly somewhere else first. The impatient woman on the other end asked where, and Lydia answered, *Seattle, Washington.*

June

Outside, the ocean crashes. She is dressed, her linen jacket is still on, and the bed she lies on is made. Something wakes her, and as her body tenses, she opens her eyes long enough to recognize the room, see the faintest light coming from behind the blinds. I'm here, she thinks, and relaxes again into the mattress. She pulls the pillow closer and tucks her legs toward her chest as she falls back to sleep.

The screen door slams. It is morning. The wooden folding chair she has fallen asleep on is now covered in dew. She is damp and her bones ache and he has come back. She stands and stretches and steps out of the tent onto the lawn where she met Luke four years ago when he came to clear fallen limbs after a tropical storm had blown them everywhere. *It's a disaster,* she said that day, and he stopped and said, amused but with a gentle authority, as if he were speaking to a child, *Oh, it's not so bad. Not really.* She remembers seeing his face for the first time and how thrown she was. How she reacted as she had before with a sculpture or installation or painting so exquisite and so stirring that she could not take it all in at once. It was the same with Luke. Eyebrow, forearm, cheekbone, neck, lower lip, eyes, bicep, mole. And the most beautiful brown skin. She had never been so struck by the physical appearance of a man before. Women, on rare occasion. Some collision of hair and skin and angle of light amid an origami of fabric and jewelry. But in faded green T-shirt and worn Levi's, this man who had come to clear branches away presented a riddle of bone and skin and eyes that left June speechless. *Oh, no, it's a disaster all right,* she remembers saying again, and how before he spoke, he smiled.

Crossing the lawn, she can see them both as they were, standing in a mess of fallen branches, the moment before meeting. Only now, damp with dew and stiff from strange sleep, does she recognize how unlikely and lucky that moment was, how she has until now taken it for granted, remembered Luke's arrival with a kind of regret, experienced his staying as a disruption, a complication, as if love were an inconvenience thrust on her, uninvited. She had welcomed him as a disaster and she was wrong. She has wasted this time and she has held him away.

When she has crossed half the distance between the tent and the house, she wants to call out to him and nearly does, but it is early and everyone is still asleep. She will be there soon, she tells herself. Through the porch door and into the house—the kitchen, the bedroom, the living room, the bathroom, wherever he is. Soon, she will find him, and for once she will not worry or be annoyed or impatient or afraid.

She hears him moving quickly through the house. He has shouted something but she is too far away to hear. It sounds like her name.

She will ask him to forgive her. And she will say yes.

Lydia

The road to Moclips from Aberdeen hugs the shore, but nothing is visible through the fog. The heavyset, young woman driving the cab said it would take forty-five minutes, but with zero visibility she's slowed to a crawl and they've been on the road for over an hour. The girl introduced herself as Reese and wears a brown bandanna wrapped simply around what looks like a shaved head. The cab smells like cigarette smoke and oranges, and Lydia feels nauseated. Madonna is singing one of her first pop songs, about dressing someone up in her love, *all over, all over*. Is it possible she heard that song for the first time over thirty years ago? At the Tap with Earl? Later? Outside, the world is as gray and white and featureless as it was when she got on the bus in Seattle after taking a cab from the airport. It never occurred to her to rent a car until Reese asked why she hadn't. Lydia wonders if everyone who flies in airplanes rents cars when they land. Has her life been so sheltered in Wells that she has no idea how the world actually works? Guess so, she thinks as she runs her hand over the top of her suitcase, where the folders with Luke's report cards and photos and newspaper clippings are tucked into the front pocket. The suitcase is one she bought the day before at the hospital thrift shop. It was three dollars and has wheels and a collapsible handle, and besides the chubby stars drawn across the top in gold Magic Marker, it's as good as new. It's the first suitcase she's ever had, and rolling it through the Hartford airport gave her an embarrassed but giddy feeling of playing the part of a stewardess on a TV show or movie. The bus driver in Seattle asked her to store the case in the luggage compartment, but she refused and said she'd hold it in her lap if she had to, which is what she did for three hours as the crowded bus rattled down the coast to Aberdeen. Though she had been drowsy on the bus, she was afraid to fall asleep for fear someone would steal it or lift her purse. But alone now in the back of the taxi, with the familiar bubblegum sounds of Madonna in the eighties, she drifts in and out of sleep. She sees Silas dragging rocks from the woods behind the fields at June's house. He lays them on vast blue plastic tarps, the kind that people in Wells use to cover woodpiles, and drags them across the high grass toward the charred site where the house had stood. She sees the enormous pile of large rocks he has amassed. It must be three stories high and nearly as wide. There are clearly more than enough rocks to build a house, but Silas is not satisfied, and after he tosses a new load from the blue tarp onto the pile, he goes back across the field and into the woods to find more. Lydia calls out to him but he cannot hear her. He is determined and he is deaf to the world, and the blue tarp flaps behind him like a great cape.

Almost there, Reese says gently from the driver's seat, Annie Lennox now barely audible in the speakers. Lydia brushes lint that has gathered on the front of her dress, a black wrap she found at Caldor's in Torrington almost fifteen years ago and which she's worn only three times: to Luke's graduation from high school, his hearing in Beacon, and his funeral. This trip felt formal, serious, like the other occasions, and so she wore it. Also, it is her best and there is still a leftover desire for June's approval from the first few times they met. Lydia had never seen June in anything more formal than jeans and khakis and skirts, but she imagined her having lived a fancy life in New York and London with dresses and jewelry and elaborate shoes. The more lint she picks from the dress, the more she sees, so she stops and looks out the window. It has been less than a week since she read Mimi's note, which started, *Dear Lydia, We thought you'd want to know where June was living,* and only a few days more since Silas appeared at her door. Maybe if these events had happened months or even weeks apart she might have felt less urgency about seeing June, maybe she would have flown to Washington after seeing George in Atlanta and not the other way around. But from the moment Lydia folded Mimi's note after reading it, she knew the only thing that mattered was finding June.

She knew if she dialed the number on the motel stationery and asked to speak to June, she risked losing her again. The only thing she could do was turn up at her door, just as June had at hers three years ago.

After Silas told her what he had to say early that morning, more than feeling relieved to discover that it was not anger or blame that most likely drove June away, she felt ashamed. She'd assumed June believed what most people in town believed: that Luke was to blame. She imagined into her dismissal and flight everything but the one thing she knew best: guilt. Knowing what weighed on top of June's grief made Lydia feel close to her again. She knew what it was like to take responsibility for calamity. She knew what it was like to live with regret. But what June carried now was much heavier; so heavy that when Lydia read Mimi's note, she knew she had to leave immediately. What she had to tell June would not replace the losses, but it would make clear what had happened and let her know that neither she nor Luke had been at fault. That Lydia could do this for June gave her something she had not felt since Luke was an infant: a clear purpose, a fierce protective love that ran on adrenaline and eliminated all other concerns or desires. She would go to June and nothing else mattered.

Reese pulls off a two-lane road into a short, sand-covered driveway that opens to a parking lot. Fog hides the place, and the only thing Lydia can see are dim white lights on either side of a door. They glow as if underwater. As the cab pulls to a stop, she has a feeling of arriving somewhere she will be for a while. A flight was booked a week from now to Atlanta, but she knows she will not be going there soon. George will be there as he has, miraculously, been all these years and eventually she will find him. In the meantime, she will stay in this foggy motel for as long as she is needed.

After she's paid Reese the fare and checked in at the office, a red-haired, middle-aged woman tells Lydia to follow her. She rolls her suitcase behind her as they walk down the cement path along a white, one-story building. Once they stop at a gray door with a black number 6 painted on it, the woman from the office lingers. Lydia can't tell if she's being protective or nosy or both. Eventually she walks away, and as she does, she reminds Lydia that if she needs anything at all, she'll be in the office.

Lydia steps forward and knocks lightly on the door. There is no answer, no movement or sound coming from the room, so she knocks again, this time with force. A creak of bedsprings is followed by silence, then a slow clicking and unlatching of locks. The door swings open and there she is, June. Lydia's legs tingle and she exhales an unexpected breath of relief, as if a part of her had secretly believed she'd made this woman up, that all of it, the life that had preceded this very moment was something she'd invented. But here was June. Proof of something, even though the woman in the doorway of this motel room was a faded version of the one Lydia remembered. Despite wearing precisely the same clothes she'd worn the last time she saw her, rushing from the church after Luke's funeral, June is almost unrecognizable. She is smaller than every memory Lydia has, and seeing her now is like what she's heard about seeing celebrities in person, how they are diminished by real life. Her arms are still and at her sides, and she looks at Lydia as if she has been caught breaking something fragile and costly. She lets go of the door, steps back. Lydia struggles to speak. *June,* she whispers, almost as if she's convincing herself of her identity. June places one foot behind her and then the other and half steps backward to the edge of the bed. She sits down, slowly, and pulls a white pillow to her lap. Lydia steps inside the room—it is neat as a pin, dark, and appears as if no one has lived here. She crosses to the bed and sits next to June. She smells the faintest lilac and remembers asking her over a year ago what perfume she wore, and June smiled and answered, *It's a little scent called menopause.* That June, the one who could occasionally, though not often, shake off her seriousness with a joke, and who could do the same for Lydia, was nowhere near this somber motel room. The one in her place, the one who has not spoken since she opened the door, sits and pinches the ends of a pillow with fingers that have clipped but unmanicured nails. Strangely, for Lydia, the silence between them is not awkward. It is a comfort to be so near June, to have found her, and that she hasn't run. For the first time, Lydia hears the ocean. It is as if a stereo switch has just been thrown and from speakers blare the sound of crashing waves. She smells the sea air and breathes it in, deeply. The nausea from before has gone and with it her fatigue. She turns to June and looks at her. Her hair is longer than she's seen it before and pulled loosely behind her in a knot of tumbling blond hair that is now dominated by silver at the roots. She is thinner, her face is gaunt, and at the edges of her tightly shut mouth, frown lines curl and splinter toward her jaw. Lydia tries to remember June's voice again but cannot. Tears begin to fall from Lydia's eyes, the first since the days just before and after the funerals last year. Over the sound of the ocean, she says to herself as much as to June, *I've missed you.* She carefully puts her arm around June's thin shoulders and they both startle from the shock of physical contact. It has been a long time since either has touched anyone. *They are gone,* Lydia says without thinking, surprised to hear the words. *They are gone,* she says again, more loudly, as if saying it with June, now, makes the fact official, finally true. For a long while, they are silent. Lydia eventually finds the bathroom, and when she returns, she gently pulls June's closest hand from the pillow to her lap.

Nine months ago, this same hand forbid her to speak, but now, here, Lydia caresses it softly. *There is so much I want to tell you,* she says, and as she does, she remembers Winton, the only person she's spoken to for more than a few moments all year. She describes that first phone call, how aware and yet how stupid she was, and how lonely. *I am a weak woman,* she whispers, and then repeats the words softly a few times. *Always have been.* As the words leave her, she can see out the window to the ocean. The last time she saw waves on a beach was when she and Earl went to Atlantic City for their honeymoon. These are taller, more majestic and powerful. She watches them rise and collapse in bursts of white foam, and as she does, she feels something leave her. She can't name it, but it was with her always, and with the words she has just spoken, it has gone.

Lydia remains still and matches her breathing to June's. They sit side by side on the bed and Lydia can feel her hand, with June's, dampen with sweat, but neither of them let go. Before she says anything about Silas, she remembers him at her apartment a week ago, speaking too fast, without inhaling, making no sense. It would take almost an hour before she truly understood what he was so desperately trying to say. When she finally did understand, she was furious—at him, for letting everyone blame Luke, for not going back in the house; at June, for not fixing that stove years before; and at herself for never insisting June do so even though Lydia had stood before the old thing herself many times shaking her head when it refused to light or to stop ticking. They were all to blame, she thought, trying to calm down. She and Silas sat on her couch for hours. She stood to go to bed several times, but each time he did not budge. So she sat with him in the bright living room, quiet. There was too much to make sense of, too much to say, so she said nothing. Eventually, she fell asleep, and when she woke and saw him curled against the sofa cushion, she could hear him sobbing. She pulled him toward her, shook his young shoulders gently, and told him it wasn't his fault, that it wasn't anybody's. She remembers his terrified eyes searching her face. It was between midnight and dawn and the day before had been a doozy, but nothing surprised her more than what she felt in that moment: needed. It was the last thing she expected. Through a mess of tears and mucus and yawning, Silas mumbled, *I'm sorry,* over and over. After a while, he slouched into the sofa, tucked his chin against his chest, and slept. Lydia watched his body rise and fall with his breathing, the lightly pimpled skin of his face agitate and twitch in response to whatever he was dreaming. Here was someone she understood. Someone alive but destroyed. She knew she could do nothing to bring her own boy back, stop him from turning whatever knob he turned or flipping whatever switch he flipped that morning, nor could she undo the mistakes she'd made when he was alive, but she might be able to help this boy. And with what he had just told her, she might be able to do the same for June.

And so she came here. *There is someone I want to tell you about,* she says. June does not move, nor does she signal in any way that she is listening. Still, Lydia continues. She tells her about Silas—who he is, who his parents are, that he worked for Luke, how he followed her, and what he said the night he turned up at her door. She tells this last part slowly, carefully, with as much detail as she can remember.

June does not respond to anything Lydia says, but when she finishes speaking, she pulls Lydia's hand slowly toward her face. June extends each finger and presses the palm against her cheek. She covers Lydia's hand with both of hers and presses gently at first and then with more pressure. As she does, June's torso and head glide downward, her feet curling behind her onto the bed, her head and shoulders resting in Lydia's lap. Neither speaks. With her free hand, Lydia gently strokes the top of June's head, brushes a few strands of hair from her face, one, then another, and then spreads her hand across her clear brow. June's breathing slows, her body loosens, and soon she is asleep. A black plastic alarm clock ticks the seconds with a blue wand. Lydia hears every one.

Cissy

I said I'd marry them and I did. I'd done it twice before: once for my nephew and his nineteen-year-old girlfriend, and the other time for a couple my sister Pam sold a house to in Ocean Shores. Rebecca and Kelly had been together a long time, but now that it was legal in the eyes of the governor, they wanted the piece of paper. Fine with me.

Compared to some weddings I've seen, Rebecca and Kelly's was small. Just the two of them; Will's family: Dale, Mimi, Pru, and Mike; Kelly's brothers and nephews and a few cousins. June was there, too. She came with Lydia, who showed up a month before. She landed in Seattle and took a bus to Aberdeen and hired a taxi to take her from there. When I saw Kelly walking a busty, dark-haired woman rolling a carry-on suitcase behind her toward Room 6, I knew right away who she was. June didn't tell me much about Luke's mother, just that she'd had a rough road with men, including her son. She described her once as a small-town Elizabeth Taylor, which is exactly what the woman heading toward Room 6 looked like. I stayed away from June's room for a couple days. Eventually, I came around to clean and bring a thermos of split pea, which is the only thing she eats besides those bags of peanuts she gets down at the gas station.

When Ben died, I went to my sister's kitchen and stayed there for months. I roasted everything I could find at Swanson's Grocery—hams, chickens, turkeys, pork roasts, potatoes—you name it. I baked dinner rolls and popovers and ate my way through cakes and pies and cookies I'd bake in the morning and eat at night after dinner. When my clothes started to pinch and I couldn't button my jeans anymore, I asked Ellie Hillworth for a job at the Moonstone. She and Bud were well into their seventies by then and had been trying to sell the place, so another hand on deck was welcome. Cleaning rooms and running trash to the Dumpster got me out of the kitchen, at least between the hours of nine and three, and after a while I settled into making pots of soup on the weekends and now and again a batch of orange drop cookies. That's how it's been for years.

Not long after June showed up at the Moonstone, half-dead and ready to go all the way, I brought her a thermos of squash soup. Never asked if I could. Just left it on the dresser in her room with a spoon and a folded paper towel for a napkin. She didn't touch it. She didn't touch the split pea I left a few days later either. But I kept on leaving the thermos, and after a while I could tell a little bit was missing when I'd pick it up the next morning. It never came back empty, but I took what was gone as a sign; that even if she didn't know it herself, she was choosing to live.

Rough as life can be, I know in my bones we are supposed to stick around and play our part. Even if that part is coughing to death from cigarettes, or being blown up young in a house with your mother watching. And even if it's to be that mother. Someone down the line might need to know you got through it. Or maybe someone you won't see coming will need you. Like a kid who asks you to let him help clean motel rooms. Or some ghost who drifts your way, hungry. And good people might even ask you to marry them. And it might be you never know the part you played, what it meant to someone to watch you make your way each day. Maybe someone or something is watching us all make our way. I don't think we get to know why. It is, as Ben would say about most of what I used to worry about, none of my business.

Some of the old-timers around here got worked up when Kelly and Rebecca came in and cleaned up the Moonstone. Even my sister Pam, who sold the place to them, wrinkled her nose. But like most things, what seemed important and wrong on one day could barely be remembered the next. Probably, there will always be wrinkled noses, folks who make jokes about the Moonstone dykes or the little boy on the rez who likes to wear his mom's earrings, or me, the half-breed, bastard bitch who lives with her sisters. It stops when we die and goes on for those we leave behind. All we can do is play our parts and keep each other company.

June and Lydia will stay here for as long as they need to. I will bring them soup and watch them come back to life, and at night I will lie in the room I grew up in and listen to my sisters open and close doors, flush toilets, and climb the stairs. In the morning I will hear their voices in the kitchen and smell the brewing coffee before I open my eyes.

Rebecca and Kelly will wear the rings I watched them put on their fingers when they said their vows. And together they will get old. The Landises will come back every year. I will make up their rooms and bring them cookies for as long as I can, and when I can't anymore, they will still come, with children and grandchildren, girlfriends and boyfriends and spouses. They will knock on our door and I will be there, crooked and old, and one day they will knock and I will be gone. And every time they come, they will tell those who don't know the story of the young man who was a boy here, who went away and came home and went away, who cleaned rooms and carved a canoe and on its prow painted the faces of a family. And the stories will change and the canoe will become a headboard and the family will be mermaids and the rooms will be mansions. And no one will remember us, who we were or what happened here. Sand will blow across Pacific Avenue and against the windows of the Moonstone, and new people will arrive and walk down the beach to the great ocean. They will be in love, or they will be lost, and they will have no words. And the waves will sound to them as they did to us the first time we heard them.

Acknowledgments

For much more than can be described here, great thanks to Jennifer Rudolph Walsh, Raffaella De Angelis, Tracy Fisher, Cathryn Summerhayes, Karen Kosztolnyik, Jennifer Bergstrom, Louise Burke, Wendy Sheanin, Carolyn Reidy, Jennifer Robinson, Michael Selleck, Lisa Litwack, Paula Amendolara, Charlotte Gill, Becky Prager, Chris Clemans, Jillian Buckley, Kassie Evashevski, Martine Bellen, John Gall, Kim Nichols, Sean Clegg, Emma Sweeney, Adam McLaughlin, Cy O'Neal, Jill Bialosky, Susannah Meadows, Stacey D'Erasmo, Sarah Shun-lien Bynum, Heidi Pitlor, Pat Strachan, Isabel Gillies, Courtney Hodell, Jean Stein, Robin Robertson, Luiz Schwarcz, Kimberly Burns, and to Alan Shapiro for writing a great poem, and Haven Kimmel for singling out the six words that planted the seed all those years ago.

Center Point Large Print
600 Brooks Road / PO Box 1
Thorndike, ME 04986-0001 USA

(207) 568-3717

US & Canada:
1 800 929-9108
www.centerpointlargeprint.com

LARGE PRINT
Clegg, Bill.
Did you ever have a family